Mischief in Moonstone Series, Novella 1: When Rudolph was Kidnapped

By Christine DeSmet

Writers Exchange E-Publishing
http://www.writers-exchange.com

Mischief in Moonstone Series, Novella 1: When Rudolph was Kidnapped
Copyright 2016, 2023, 2025 Christine DeSmet
Writers Exchange E-Publishing
PO Box 372
ATHERTON QLD 4883

Cover Art by: Sandy Cummins

Published by Writers Exchange E-Publishing
http://www.writers-exchange.com

Originally published in **SMALL GIFTS, the first Jewels of the Quill Christmas anthology**
Released September 2005
Edited by Carrie S. Masek, Jane Toombs, and Karen Wiesner

Chapter 1

"He bit me, Miss Hagan! Marcus bit me! And he socked me in the gut!" Gretchen Johnson fell onto the snow in her pink snowsuit and boots, kicking and bawling as if in the throes of a theatrical death.

Ordinarily, Crystal Hagan would count to ten before charging into the middle of a first-graders' fray, but not when the thermometer placed the wind chill factor at twenty-below zero earlier that morning in Moonstone, Wisconsin. With the weather so bad, she only brought her thirteen students out for ten minutes right after lunch, just enough to help them settle down for the afternoon. Otherwise, they acted like Mexican jumping beans, though Marcus, ever challenging her, had reminded her once that those were actually moths trying to break out of their cocoons.

Crystal called out, "Marcus, come here this instant or you're not going with us to see Rudolph this afternoon."

Marcus stood atop the snow mountain the plow had created after two feet of snow hit recently in Moonstone, a town of three hundred huddled on the shore of Lake Superior. Other boys and a couple of girls allowed in

Marcus's kingdom popped their heads over the snow mountain. They made Crystal smile. They looked like a row of baby dragons, but instead of fire breathing out of them, their mouths and noses spewed frost onto the icy air.

Looking up at the mountain of snow taller than she, Crystal said, "All of you play nice or Santa won't be coming either." She hated using that trump card, but teachers could get desperate. She still had her fingers crossed that Randy Mellen didn't back out on this date, too. His dentistry practice in Superior kept him too busy as of late, but when he'd called last night to postpone their date, he'd promised to make up for it by showing up in a Santa Claus suit today and tomorrow for the kids.

Crystal flagged Marcus down off the mountain, grabbed the little boy's arm and marched him over to Gretchen. "Show me where he bit you, Gretch."

Through blubbering and tears, and sucking at the air, the six-year-old girl finally said, "I don't remember."

Marcus broke into laughter. "See? She's lying. Maybe she can't go see Rudolph because she lied. No Christmas presents, Gretchy Vetchy."

"Stop that. Santa brings presents to everybody who's nice. It's time to go inside. Line up, everybody."

Somehow, she knew Marcus would create another disaster. He had a way of stirring up the other children. She thought about canceling their walk across the town Square from the school to see Rudolph. The morning hadn't started well, and for the first time in years, trouble brewed over the live animal crèche created every holiday season for the village by Crystal.

Only a few hours earlier, before school started, she'd pulled the livestock trailer with her four-wheel drive Grand Cherokee into place on the snow-covered lawn area of the mansion long known as the North Pole. When she dropped off her reindeer and the donkey she'd met with protesters--the couple volunteering to play Mary and Joseph, and Mayor Bob Winters.

Pulling down the thick, woolen stocking cap over her long blonde hair, she got out of the truck to face Jeri and Kirk Kaminski who rushed up to her before even one of her tall boots sunk into the snow. She could barely see their faces, what with the fur hoods pulled tight against the nippy weather. Jeri's breath had created a ring of white frost on the blue woolen scarf she wore wrapped around her face.

"Enough is enough. I'm not standing out here on this property any more freezing my toes off. I want to be paid."

Not a very saintly thing for "Mary" to say, Crystal thought. "We all volunteer. I don't get paid to do this, Jeri. But the kids love it. Everybody loves it."

Kirk shook his head. More flumes of steam hit the air. "I'm out of a job."

"I'm sorry. I didn't know."

"Because of the old fart who owns the land under this snow right here." His thumb pointed at the mansion behind where they stood. "If he thinks he can lay me off, then watch me freeze my toes off from behind his warm windows, he's got a screw loose."

With that, they got into their pickup truck and drove away. Just like that she'd lost Mary and Joseph. Confused about what was going on, she didn't have long to wait for clarification.

Mayor Bob Winters, his portly girth covered in a camouflage snowmobile suit and blaze orange stocking cap, had trundled up to her next. He'd turned sixty recently without grace. The scarlet capillaries on his face from too many brandy old-fashions had turned to a shade of purple this morning. "No more live animals, Crystal. Take them home. Now."

At five-foot, ten inches, she stood eye-to-eye with the mayor. "Come on, Bob, we've done this Nativity for years. What's going on?"

"These are what's going on." He took several loose papers out of a pocket and waved them at her. "Letters of complaint. Mostly about me, for condoning such a thing."

She ripped the letters out of his hand and perused them. "They're all in the same handwriting. Bob, I'm sure it's just a prankster. Nobody's ever complained about the Nativity scene. Besides, we're on private land."

"That could be who's behind this. Old Henri LeBarron. The old coot is probably certifiable. Gotta be some reason he hasn't come out of that mansion in five years."

The Nativity scene was her very own idea to help make the town festive and attract more shoppers every year on the Saturday two weeks before Christmas. Knowing she couldn't construct the small, three-sided, roofed manger on public land, she'd sent a letter to Henri LeBarron, now in his eighties, asking his permission to use the generous front lawn of his mansion where she and Bob stood that morning. The estate overlooked Lake Superior in the back, though nobody she knew remembered being invited to enjoy the sight. Ironically, the reclusive Henri had once played Santa for celebrations in Moonstone, but that was a couple of decades ago, when Crystal was in college and away. Now forty-three, and anchored in the harbor community, she bristled with the feeling of betrayal as she looked at the three-story home, a grand affair long ago dubbed the North Pole by children because of Henri's stint as Santa. Indeed, the place looked like Santa's house. Her first graders said the detailed arches painted in red looked like eyebrows over windows and doors. They said the drifts whipped by the storm and hanging precariously over the eaves of the green roof reminded them of frosting on a giant cupcake.

She handed the letters back to Bob then went about unloading her pet reindeer and donkey. "I can't believe Henri would do this. He gave me permission years ago. I have it in writing, Bob."

"Yeah, and Kirk had an employment contract in the coal yards in the Superior harbor. Which Henri LeBarron put up for sale just yesterday then started in on downsizing the work force to make the deal look good."

"He's doing that at Christmastime?" With her hands on the halters of the animals on either side of her, she paused coming down the short ramp to stare in disbelief at Bob.

"I've been on the phone all morning. Twenty-eight families from around Moonstone are affected by the old bastard's actions. Talk about putting coal in the stockings of children literally."

"It doesn't make sense, unless Henri needs the money. But I always assumed he had all the money in the world." She looked at the mansion, the windows dark in the dim light of the winter's morning. Everybody knew Henri had sold his ownership of a Lake Superior cargo shipping business years ago. Had he run through his millions? An ugly thought struck her heart.

"You don't suppose he's going to sell the mansion, too? This has been the North Pole forever, and the last piece of private land on the entire Square. What will happen to the holiday crèche?"

The crèche had quickly become a tradition she loved doing just to see the smiles on kids and their parents' faces at the holiday. There was something about petting animals that brought out the best in people. She led Rudolph and Gracie the donkey into place inside the protective shelter of the plywood Nativity stable. With golden straw so deep it touched their bellies they would stay cozy. Both were used to the cold Wisconsin winters. Today was Friday, the trial run to acclimate them to the lean-to for tomorrow's big day when they hoped to draw shoppers to town. So far, the animals loved the adventure, while Bob did not.

He waved the anonymous letters at her again. "If I end up getting sued over this holiday display, you're going to have to pay the lawyer's fees. This dang Nativity thing on the old coot's land was your idea."

He'd stomped away, kicking at the snowbanks along the sidewalk.

Now, herding her class toward the school, she glanced over at the LeBarron home, pines flanking it in the front yard. What kind of existence did Henri have these days? Everybody saw his helper, a mysterious man called Leonard Moline, skulk in and out of the grocery store now and then, but the man was so creepy nobody engaged in talk with him, not even about the weather. Maybe Moline was behind Henri's sale of the coal yards. Certainly he had no allegiance to Moonstone or any of the other small towns dependent on ship yards and train yards coming together in Duluth-Superior. Maybe he was lobbying for Henri to move south now, where it didn't reach thirty-below at night or even have a real winter.

Despite being bundled up and wearing her thermal t-shirt and leggings under her clothes, Crystal shivered with dread. There certainly was some kind of dirty dealings going on under the innocence of the white snow. With a heavy loss of jobs, land and home values in Moonstone would plummet. Residents losing their jobs would need to move away, and they'd get next to nothing for their homes. Who would want to move here? Some Christmas season this would be.

Suddenly, Gretchen broke ranks and tackled Marcus in the snow.

"Gretchen Johnson, stop that."

But the little imp was hot for revenge. She and Marcus rolled about, snow flying as their arms and stubby legs flailed. The other students took sides as if this were a Packers-Bears game with everything on the line. "Go, Marcus! You got 'im, Gretchen! Hit him harder!"

Crystal hauled both wiggling snow figures upright. "When I ask you nicely to come in, I expect you to respect me and come along."

Marcus, in even greater theatrics than Crystal, fell backwards, playing dead in the snow. Crystal sighed. He stiffened his limbs and squeezed his face tight, an act that many first graders seemed to do as they bridged from the age of temper tantrums on store floors to discovering new curse words from older children. Crystal wasn't looking forward to that stage either. She picked up the stiff Marcus and carried him into the school. There was an advantage to being tall and tough from farm work. She could pick up a child as if he were a naughty puppy gnawing on something he shouldn't.

"Ouch!" she yelped when Marcus pulled a strand of her hair escaping from under her wool cap. "That's it."

Instead of taking a right to her classroom, she turned left and marched with him down the yellow hallway to the principal's office. This would be the third time in as many weeks that she'd end up in a meeting with Lisa and Lowell Dane, Marcus's parents. She was on the verge of calling in Gretchen's parents as well. What more could go wrong today?

Her thirteen students hung onto the jingle bell rope as Crystal led them through the snowy sidewalks across the open Square toward the holiday crèche. Each child owned one of the harness bells she'd secured with a ribbon to the rope. The bells, which she special ordered through Johnson's Hardware Store, replicated the bell the children saw in the Christmas book she had read to them earlier that week called *The Polar Express*. As was her tradition each year with her class, she told the children that if they behaved at the holiday animal display, each could take home their very own bell. Even if they didn't behave, she'd find a way to make sure each child received their special bell before the vacation break a week away, but that was her secret.

They crossed LeBarron Street, then climbed over the snowbanks to get to the sidewalk in front of the North Pole. Marcus Dane broke ranks and tore into the Nativity scene screeching, "Rudolph's gone! Somebody stole Rudolph!"

Tiny Gretchen's face turned into rivulets of tears. "We won't get any presents!"

Marcus said, "Shit, no Rudolph, no Christmas!"

"Marcus Dane, I swear I'll..." Crystal said, putting her mitten-covered hand over his mouth, not knowing what to say. She was in shock, too.

The Garcia twins, Fernando and Octavio, bawled almost in unison, their faces swarthy piles of wrinkled up misery, mouths open and showing their missing front teeth.

"Now, now, Freddy, don't cry. Octavio, we'll find Rudolph."

But Crystal panicked. She looked about the street, the Square, back to the yard of the mansion. Rudolph was nowhere in sight. Her gaze landed on a trail of boot tracks leading from the mock stable to the mansion. Before she could say anything, the quietest child in her class, Michael Lone Eagle, tugged at her coat sleeve.

"Rudolph was kidnapped, wasn't he?" Michael bit his lower lip, which was chapped and bleeding at one corner from the cold weather. "My little brother was kidnapped."

Swallowing hard and trying to think of something to say, Crystal knelt down in the snow with a tissue to wipe at Michael's face and lip, then dug out her Chapstick and rubbed it around his lips. "Try not to lick your lips, Michael. And we're going to find Rudolph."

"My brother never came home." His dark eyes grew wider, beseeching her.

"Honey, I'm very, very sorry about your brother. Let's you and me talk about that later, okay?"

Most of her charges were sobbing, one cry having triggered another. Crystal had the sense she was staring at a nest of baby birds of all colors, their mouths open in desperation for her to drop sustenance and answers into them. But she had no answers. Except for the trail to the LeBarron mansion. The urge to repeat Marcus's choice word welled up in her. How could Henri do this to the children? What had made that old coot turn on her? Or was it creepy Leonard Moline?

Forcing on a smile, she gathered up the children by shaking the rope to make the bells jingle. "Class, now listen. I'm betting Rudolph went into the woods to round up the other reindeer for Santa's sleigh. That's all. Remember tomorrow? The sleigh rides you can take around the Square?"

"But that's with a horse," Gretchen peeped between a sniffle.

Crystal counted to five. "Who do you think gives the horse directions on how to pull the sleigh? Rudolph. That must be where he is now, teaching the horse."

That mollified them. They hurried back to the school. But when she stood next to the buses at three p.m. counting noses, she was missing Michael Lone Eagle. She'd left him putting on his boots at his locker.

She found Michael inside his locker, legs and feet drawn up so that he was almost hidden under his coat that still hung above him on its hook. Crystal held out her hand.

"Hey there, young man, it's time to go home. The bus is waiting."

"I don't want to go home."

Worry ebbed through Crystal. She knelt down, pushing her hair back over her shoulders. She thought about the mysterious kidnapped brother. "Why not?"

He didn't move from the safe cocoon of the locker. He was the cutest little boy she'd ever encountered, and smart, too, the kind of kid who reminded her she had always wanted children of her own.

Michael's shoulders heaved a big sigh. "Mommy cries a lot because my brother is gone."

Crystal waited, knowing that was sometimes the best response.

He continued in a whispery voice, "His daddy is different than my daddy. His daddy took him and he never came back. Sometimes my daddy goes away for a long time, too, and I don't think he's going to come back either. If I tell Mommy about Rudolph, it'll make her cry because maybe my brother won't get presents. I don't care if I get presents, but I want Rudolph and Santa to find my brother."

Relief washed over Crystal. The half-brother was likely okay and with his own father. But Michael was missing his father. He worked construction which often took him long distances away from home because jobs were scarce on the nearby Indian reservation as well as around Moonstone.

She patted Michael's knee and gave him a wide smile. "That's so nice of you, Michael, to care that much about your brother and mother. And you know what? Your father would be very proud of you for caring so much."

He looked her long and hard in the eyes, then a winsome smile curved his slim lips. He tumbled out and locked his arms around her neck in a tight hug. She couldn't breathe.

"Thank you, Miss Hagan. Please find Rudolph," he mumbled against her neck, his words tickling. "I want a boat, you know, for Christmas."

"No, I didn't know."

"A really really big one. Only Rudolph is strong enough to bring it, I'm sure."

She had to smile. She hugged him back, enjoying his little boy smell.

Already she hatched a plan to get Rudolph back from that old curmudgeon living at the North Pole. She had something she knew Henri LeBarron couldn't resist.

Chapter 2

At a little before six p.m. Crystal stood on the dark, green porch of the North Pole, her teeth chattering more from anger than the cold, though the temperature already dipped to ten below zero. Moonlight created rivers of liquid mercury across the deep snowdrifts in the side yards. Snow-draped pine trees moaned in an intermittent, whistling breeze.

Crystal shifted the secret weapon in her arms. The moonlight reflecting off the snow helped her see the doorbell button. She punched it a third time, then knocked on the red door. "Hello? Mister LeBarron?"

The door swept open with such force that it almost sucked her in.

One look at the tall man with piercing dark eyes blocking the entryway made her knees want to buckle. This was not a wizened, elderly, frail man. He stood ramrod straight and taller than she, a rock wall from his lugged boots up to broad shoulders. Muscular arms were accentuated by a bulky, cream-colored cable-stitch sweater. Denim jeans covered legs set in a determined stance. Wavy chestnut hair sported just enough gray at the sides to give him the edge of a Lake Superior ship's captain, one who didn't care to be disturbed.

Her armpits grew damp. "Uh, I was hoping to talk with Mr. LeBarron, with Henri."

"Well you can't," he said in a low timbre while beginning to close the door in her face.

"Hey, hold on. I brought him this."

Those dark eyes, so like steady gun barrels, looked down his nose. "What might that be?"

Ah, a foot in the door, she thought. She held out the pan wrapped in a blanket, embarrassed by how much her hands shook. "It's chocolate pudding cake."

"Pudding?"

"No, cake. You see, you stir all this stuff up and when it bakes, what happens is the top bakes like a cake, but then when you cut into it, you find hot chocolate sauce in the bottom, which is great when you use a spoon to drizzle it over the baked portion and put cream on top. I brought cream. It's in a carton in my coat pocket."

The door slammed shut.

Her mouth dropped open. Then a fire rose through her middle. Echoes of her crying kids plagued her. She knocked hard with a fist on the door. When that didn't rouse the man, she kicked the door with her boot for good measure.

This time a porch light came on over her head. Mr. Cable Sweater Man opened the door again, crossing his arms across the wide chest. She was about to speak when a loose swatch of his thick hair sprung loose to tickle his forehead in a way that made her mouth go dry.

He squinted at her. "Henri's not accepting visitors."

Think fast. "Is Leonard home?" she asked, frustration mounting. "Or have you murdered him, too?"

He unfolded his arms. "Excuse me?"

She clung to the cake pan. "A weak joke. Sorry. This pudding cake is still warm. It's Henri's favorite thing in the whole world."

"And how do you know that?"

"Henri always bought my mother's chocolate pudding cake when he stopped by the church fundraisers. But that was years ago. Now he buys mine, but he doesn't know it because Leonard comes over to the fundraiser to buy things."

When he stared at her in disbelief yet, she added, "My mother's Jennifer Hagan. I'm Crystal Hagan."

A grin eased onto his face. The rifle intensity of the eyes melted a little. He took the pan from her. "I'm sorry. Come in. I thought you were some street person giving me a line so I'd give you money."

"We don't have street people in Moonstone. It's too cold." She stepped into the front hall, a massive room the size of her entire log house. Warm air prickled at the beginnings of frostbite in her cheeks as she looked about, mesmerized by the austere beauty. "It looks exactly the same, even after twenty years."

"On what occasion were you here?"

"Henri hosted a reception to raise money for college scholarships and there was a cake walk involved. My mother and I--"

"Brought chocolate pudding cakes." The glint in his eyes...made her hungry in a way that embarrassed her. She really needed to insist Randy keep their dates more often.

"Yes." She averted her gaze to the reception hall and its original paintings of Lake Superior ships and wildlife. The polished maple wood floor in its unusual spiral design reflected sparkling light dripping from probably the only chandelier in all of Moonstone and the county.

With a slight limp, Mr. Cable Sweater Man walked over to a marble table under a portrait of a younger Henri LeBarron and set down the pudding cake.

"You must be...?" She hadn't seen Peter since she was in first grade and he in eighth. His eyes and the strong set of his jaw matched the man in the portrait.

He held out a hand. "Peter LeBarron. I'm sorry for my behavior. Back home, the panhandlers can get to be a problem."

"It's really you? After all these years?"

He laughed. "Don't make me sound so old. I'm only fifty-one and still able to do a hundred pushups at a time. Want proof?"

She giggled. "No. I believe you." With that physique, she imagined him being able to do anything he set his mind to.

She took off her double set of mittens to shake his hand. "Welcome back."

His strong grip and the shine in his eyes gave her the sense she'd follow him anywhere. Uncomfortable with his hypnotic power, she stepped back.

"Sorry for staring," he said. "I can't believe the little squirt in the pigtails who used to kick me in the shins at recess is all grown up. And looking beautiful. What I can see of you."

He made her laugh again. Still hidden under her stocking cap, she looked down at the heavy coat, nylon wind pants over her blue jeans, and boots. "It's the uniform until April."

"You should try Phoenix. It was seventy-five degrees yesterday when I left. If only I could convince my father to move there." A cloud haunted the edges of his eyes.

"Henri's okay?"

"Oh, yes. And no. He's getting on, is all."

They stood in the entry hall for an awkward moment until she recalled why she'd come. "Would it be okay if I talked with Henri? I could take him the pudding cake, if he's not able to walk--"

"I'm sorry, he doesn't care for visitors. Thanks for stopping by, though." Peter limped to the door, opening it for her to leave.

She didn't budge, her heart beating out of rhythm. "Listen, your father kidnapped Rudolph and I want him back. Well, 'her' actually."

He slammed the door shut against the cold air, but she still shivered at the intensity deepening the Phoenix tan. He said, "If you're here because you're suing my father, please pick up that cake and leave."

"I saw the tracks. All the way from the Nativity scene to this house. Your father took Rudolph this afternoon and I want him back."

Then something magical happened. She watched Peter go from being angry to booming laughter that bounced off the shiny wood floor to echo up the open staircase. "Oh I see. The pudding cake is a bribe, a trade. Chocolate cake for a reindeer. Oh my, that's the funniest thing I've ever heard." The broad shoulders shook with his chuckles.

"Seems like a good deal to me."

"There's only one problem."

"What is that?"

"My father never stole your reindeer. I did. I kidnapped Rudolph. And I'm not giving him back."

What had he just said? He admitted it? Fury fishtailed up her spine. "What do you want with a reindeer?"

"Actually, my father asked me to kidnap the reindeer for him. He's holding the reindeer for ransom." Peter kept chuckling.

"This is no joke, Peter."

"I'm not joking."

"I don't have any money."

Shaking his head, but still smiling, Peter walked back to the front door, then leaned against it with one hand on the doorknob, obviously ready to dismiss her. "Dad doesn't want your money. I suspect he'd even give you some if it'd help matters along. Here's his deal: Dad wants the mayor to agree not to run for re-election this spring or ever again, and you can have your reindeer back."

She choked. "Now I see what's going on. It's not enough that your father's selling off all his property and putting everybody out of work right at Christmastime, but now he wants to get rid of the mayor who speaks up against him doing so. I want my reindeer."

"I want my mayor."

She let go with a string of curse words not unlike what little Marcus had said earlier in the day.

In response, Peter's long arm scooped her up. He escorted her outside the door, which managed to spank her butt when it shut like a punctuation mark. The lock clicked. The porch light snapped off.

The frigid breeze brought the sting of reality to Crystal. She shivered. Then burned with rage. Fists formed inside her mittens. Poor Rudolph, docile as a puppy, was ensconced somewhere inside the LeBarron mansion. The aging outbuildings had long ago been removed from the property, so the only place the animal could be was inside.

She clomped off the porch and back to her truck. Peter LeBarron and his father weren't getting away with this ridiculous blackmail. Never mind she'd tried to bribe them. Now she had to find a way to get back inside that mansion, with or without permission.

Over chicken dinner, which Leonard Moline served in the dining room of the second floor suite belonging to Henri, Peter took careful stock of his aging father. They faced each other across the ends of the table. His father had a full head of silver hair, but it needed a trim. He wore a brown plaid flannel shirt frayed at the cuffs. His appearance, Peter guessed, was carefully planned to irritate the son. Peter knew the game. It was why after college he'd never come back except for the briefest of weekend visits around holidays. Already he was counting the minutes until his flight left Duluth.

But Crystal Hagan's information troubled Peter. His gut recognized he may need to stay beyond the weekend to clear up a few matters.

"Why didn't you tell me you were selling off the coal yard in Superior, Dad?" After Crystal had left, Peter made phone calls. He found out that his father's actions had already put several Moonstone residents out of work.

"Why shouldn't I sell? It's never been of interest to you. You're back for the other business anyway."

"Selling this house?" Peter had been duped royally, he realized now. "You timed my visit to take care of the issue of the house with the sale of the coal yard. You figured I'd have to finally get involved in your corporations. Am I on the mark?"

His father shrugged. With shaky hands, the elderly man battled with the chicken on his plate. Peter's throat tightened. When had his father not been able to cut a piece of tender chicken? Peter didn't know what to do. If he got up and helped, would that offend his father? He stayed seated, discomfort mounting as he watched his father's fumbling hands.

"I'm not moving back here to clean up your messes again," he said, trying to recapture the bluster the two men usually shared during Peter's visits.

To Peter's surprise, the older man didn't say anything. Instead, defeated by the chicken, he switched to scooping up the mashed potatoes. So that his father didn't see him staring at him, Peter averted his gaze to room and its heavy, maroon-colored velvet drapes shutting out the world. Behind him in the sitting area, the fireplace fizzed and crackled, matching Peter's racing thoughts. Was his father ill? How ill? When had the trembling started? Did Peter dare ask? How does a son ask about such things the first time without risking anger in return? His father had always been a fiercely proud man, not one who put up with weakness in anybody.

Peter looked about the room hoping answers would leap out at him. The drapes over the windows kept the chill at bay, but they also kept out the world and prying eyes that might look on with pity. When Peter reached for the blue Wedgwood cup with steaming coffee, a sudden flash of Crystal Hagan's bright eyes brought him an idea. Oddly enough, her plight over her reindeer eased his racing blood pressure. This was a safe subject to talk about with his father, a way to work up to asking about the important questions of health and the liquidation of a lifetime's work.

Peter put down his cup. "Do you really have that woman's reindeer hidden away?"

"You think I'm not capable of such things? I've still got two good legs and my wits."

But why had they been served dinner upstairs instead of in the lower dining hall? "Dad, when was the last time you went down the staircase without assistance?"

"Just today. To kidnap the reindeer."

"Dad, I'm worried about you."

"Since when? You fly in and out a couple of times a year and hurry back to Phoenix to push your papers. You call that work? I used to shovel coal by hand..."

How was it that a parent could make a grown child feel mad and guilty at the same time, and in a flash? Peter let both emotions wash over him. He'd carried guilt all his life about not having a better relationship with his father. But it was complicated. At the funeral for his mother, a teenage Peter had accused his father of killing her. Peter had apologized for his words, but it hurt that Henri, through all these years, had never offered an apology for actions that led to the loss of Peter's mother. The events surrounding her death were locked inside an imaginary box that sat between the two men. They could never reach each other without first stumbling over the box, so neither dared to reach out.

Peter watched his father sipping his coffee, wrestling with tremors in his hand, a hand that had once worked machinery that moved coal between ships and boxcars. As a boy, Peter remembered going with his father a few times to the Lake Superior port. Henri always had to be out with the employees, getting coal dust under his fingernails. Looking at his father now, Peter wondered if selling the coal yard would be the worst mistake of Henri's life. Running an empire gave Henri LeBarron purpose in life; without it, he would waste away from boredom. He'd surely blame his son for that, too. Peter wasn't about to let that happen. He didn't need more guilt to carry around.

Peter was faced with dealing with a coal yard, people out of work, and a kidnapped reindeer. What was his next move? Wind howled outside. He reached for his cup again. The liquid's warmth shimmying through him reminded him of Crystal again. He'd played along with her reindeer story out of an impulse he still couldn't quite figure out. He thought it all some joke. He was mortified later when he mentioned the incident to his father, who admitted to kidnapping the beast. After much searching, Peter hadn't found Rudolph. And his father refused to reveal the hiding place.

"What do you know about Crystal Hagan?" he asked Henri.

"Why?"

"She brought you a chocolate pudding cake, Dad. You have the hots for her?"

"Damn sure better wash your mouth out with soap before you go to bed."

Peter looked twice, but yup, that was a blush on his old man's face. Peter laughed, which sparked hiked eyebrows on his father's face. There hadn't been much laughter in this house over the past few years. Certainly Leonard Moline didn't look like a comic who could spew jokes. Peter made a mental note to check out Leonard's background more thoroughly. He'd also question him about the missing reindeer.

"Crystal could be trouble for you, Dad. I don't think she's going to give up on this kidnapping of Rudolph."

"I thought you gave her the boot."

"Not everybody owns a reindeer. It's probably worth a pretty penny to her. She might take this into a nuclear war."

Henri scoffed, then sipped more coffee. "She's just a first-grade teacher. How much harm can a teacher of little kids do to me? Nah, she wants that reindeer back for those little tykes. She'll find a way to get Mayor Winters out of my hair."

"Something tells me you could finally lose your hair over this."

"That mayor wants my property for condos!"

"But if you're selling the house, what do you care?"

"He'll fill the backyard with rows of condo apartments. You won't be able to see the lake anymore."

Peter tapped a finger on the table. "So you want to sell this place, but keep the view? Dad, this is prime lakefront property. It'll turn into a resort or condos in the blink of an eye. I don't think it's possible to keep the view."

"Find a way. Or the reindeer disappears."

Peter simmered behind clenched teeth. "Why are you doing this?"

"Doing what? Conducting business?"

"Doing all this craziness all of a sudden?" Peter's heart pounded against his chest wall. He was ever so close to asking about the trembling hands, about taking his father to a doctor. "Why the urgency to sell off the coal yard? The house? The fight with the mayor over this land? And kidnapping a reindeer? Dad, you've gone around the bend."

Henri's gaze stayed on his plate of uneaten chicken. "For you, that's nothing new. Was I not the man who killed your mother?"

It felt like a steak knife jabbed Peter's soul. "Dad, that was long ago. Please, let's just leave it there." *Locked in that box we don't want to start stumbling over.*

Henri's eyes concentrated on the shaky cup of coffee he was drawing upward toward his lips.

Leonard Moline came in then to serve them the chocolate pudding cake that he'd re-heated until it steamed hot. He set a china saucer in front of each of them. A dollop of whipped cream melted on top of the gooey cake, which floated in a pool of rich, dark chocolate sauce. One bite and Peter knew in that instant that his father was very, very wrong about Crystal Hagan. She was more than just a first-grade teacher. If she did everything as well as she baked, they were in for trouble.

Chapter 3

When Crystal parked her truck and cattle trailer in front of the LeBarron estate and the plywood stable at nine o'clock Saturday morning, the town's Square was bustling already. She smiled in outward confidence, but her nerves sent a fluttering sensation down her back, then into her stomach where the flutters wouldn't quit. Steeling herself, she put her plan in action. It took her only a few minutes to wrestle her cargo onto the porch and ring the doorbell.

To her disappointment, Leonard Moline answered the door. He poked his head out the door and peered about with his beady eyes and crooked nose, looking like a frightened crow.

"Hi," Crystal squeaked. She drew in a breath of cold air. "I'm here to give Peter LeBarron the gifts he deserves for the holiday. Can you tell him Crystal Hagan is here?"

"You're giving him these things?" Leonard pointed his nose about the porch.

"Please, Leonard, it's cold out here."

The door closed. Soon it opened again. This time Peter, hair still damp from a shower and falling over his forehead in a way that made her swallow, poked his head out.

"Crystal? What the--?"

She didn't give him a chance to shut the door in her face again. She picked up the small bale of hay bound in twine and led her donkey into the front hall. The donkey's hooves made click-clack sounds. Crystal set the bale of hay down under the chandelier.

After shutting the door, Peter gaped at her. He held a towel in one hand. The scent of his soap warred with the smell of, well, donkey.

"What the hell is this? Get this animal out of here."

Flutters from her stomach crawled into her throat. "This is Gracie. Rudolph's best friend. Since you insist on keeping Rudolph, I didn't think you'd want him to be lonely. Would you?"

"I don't know anything about reindeer and donkeys. Now get them out before my father has a heart attack."

She sat on the hay bale, which Gracie was nibbling at already. "Feed them each a wedge of hay, maybe four inches wide or so, for breakfast and lunch. For dinner, you'll want Leonard to mix ground corn with a touch of molasses or ginger snap cookies."

She hurried past him and out the door, thanking her lucky stars it was too cold for him to follow her.

He yelled from the doorway, "Get back here. Right now."

She kept on going, smiling in the frigid air at the success of her little plan. Peter LeBarron would be forking over Rudolph within minutes.

To her disappointment, and some amusement, Peter came out of the house within minutes, tugging on Gracie's lead rope. Not used to minding strangers, the donkey balked, sliding in the snow with stiffened legs while Peter pulled with all his might.

"Come on, you miserable beast, come on."

"Talk to her nice and maybe you'll get somewhere," Crystal called from where she stood next to the cattle trailer parked at the curb.

Peter stopped, puffing steam from the exertion. Bundled in heavy winter garb with only his eyes showing between a black stocking cap and a navy parka zipped up over his chin, he looked from Gracie to Crystal. His stance, like the one last evening, reminded her of his capabilities. She should run from him. But she also possessed an unreasonable urge to niggle him. What was it about this man that got her so riled up, that attracted her to all this trouble? She could, after all, just report him to the sheriff, but she had not. She'd kicked him in the shins countless times as a kid, and now had plunked a donkey in his proverbial lap. What was that about? It was as silly as Marcus and Gretchen constantly fighting.

Leaning toward Gracie's long face, and reaching out a tentative hand to pat her neck, Peter said, "Okay, girl, if you come with me I'll promise to give you all the ginger snap cookies you can possibly eat for Christmas."

Unknown to Peter, Gracie followed anybody who sweet-talked her. She began plodding next to Peter down the sidewalk.

Hiding her smile, Crystal focused on pulling the pin on the ramp in the trailer gate. "You can bring Rudolph out here anytime, too."

Peter trudged up. "I didn't take your reindeer. But my father says he did it."

Her laughter came easily. "Now that's the silliest darn thing I've ever heard. He hasn't been outside in years."

"I'm not so sure."

She glanced at him and saw honesty softening the dark eyes. "Wait a minute, you're suspicious of your own father? How could he sneak out and wrestle a reindeer? In broad daylight? In this weather?"

"It sounds odd to me, too, but he's acting odd. He shouldn't be selling all of his holdings, and there seems to be an urgency that he won't reveal."

"You need to get to the bottom of it and fast."

"Why's that?"

He started stamping his feet to keep warm. Gracie nuzzled about his coat looking for open pockets.

Crystal pulled the pin from the latch on the other side of the trailer gate, which doubled as the ramp when lowered. "I dropped in on the mayor last night. It seems the battle lines have been drawn between him and your father. The mayor wants the property for the village development, and your father wants the mayor to step down. Bob's not stepping down. No matter what happens, the kids lose because this is the last of the private property on the Square. The holiday crèche will have to go. And within the hour I've got to explain there's no Rudolph for kids wanting to get their pictures taken to send to grandmas."

"They stand out here for pictures in this cold?" He stamped some more.

"Wuss. It's getting up to zero today. We'll all be wearing shorts by the afternoon."

When he stepped over to help pull the ramp down, she stayed his gloved hand. "You have no real clue what you're doing out here, do you?"

"None whatsoever, but it seems Rudolph is in my father's clutches, so I owe you."

Her steamy breath met his frost on the air. The intimacy of sharing the very air she breathed with Peter made her swallow and step back. He took a step back as well, but his dark gaze snagged her and held tight, creating heat that steamed the air even more.

Lowering the ramp gave her a diversion and relief from his effect.

"What's that?" Peter asked.

He was peering at the fawn-colored animal facing them in the trailer. "Meet Alice. She's an alpaca."

Alice loved everybody. She trotted over to Peter right away to nose about his face with woolly lips and nostrils. Peter backed up a step, his hands out to protect himself. "She bite?"

"Of course not. I take her into nursing homes and my classroom all the time. She's even been allowed in a hospital room once." Crystal put the end of Alice's lead rope in Peter's hands. "Take her inside the stable to the right. We'll put her in Rudolph's place today."

Crystal grinned at the way Peter's hand inched out to pat Alice. He said, "Come on, girl, come with me. There you go."

Alice trotted down the incline of the ramp, then pranced around him in the snow, making Peter turn full circle to keep up with her and not get wound in the lead rope. Crystal laughed.

"Help me here," Peter said, puffing more steam. "How do I make her stop?"

He was taller than Alice, yet the dainty animal had the big man flummoxed. Crystal let Alice turn him on a fourth revolution before she stepped over to grab Alice's halter. Gracie brayed from the sidewalk out of jealousy for attention.

Peter plunked a heavy hand on Crystal's shoulder and blinked a few times. "Darn animal made me dizzy."

The pressure of Peter's strong hand gave Crystal pause, but she focused on Alice. "Alice loves to play games. When I want her to stop it or pay attention to me, I take hold of her halter and look her in the eyes."

"They're beautiful eyes."

He wasn't looking at Alice. A flush of heat chased the cold off Crystal's cheeks.

Peter said, "That's what happened to my father. Same color."

"You're flirting to distract me from marching to the North Pole and searching it myself for Rudolph."

"North Pole?"

Crystal left him with Alice so she could tie Gracie's lead rope inside the crèche's stable. "Your house. You didn't know it's called the North Pole?"

"No."

When Crystal came back for Alice, she really looked at Peter. "How can you not know that about your father? I bet you didn't know he used to play Santa Claus for the kids years ago."

"My father?" Peter's eyes went wide. "No way."

"He'd dress up and stroll around the Square and pop in and out of the stores and the diner and even the bar. He was the best Santa that Moonstone ever had."

Peter patted Alice's fuzzy neck. "Maybe you could tell the kids that Santa needed Rudolph to get ready for Christmas."

After fluffing up the straw in the stable, Crystal went to the truck and took out the fliers she'd stayed up late last night preparing. She handed a sheaf of them to Peter.

"What's this?"

He could very well see what it was, what with the picture of Rudolph at the top. She read from the flier. "Have you seen this caribou? Name is Rudolph. Four feet, eleven inches tall. Likes oatmeal cookies. Last seen being kidnapped on the LeBarron property."

A whimper came from Peter. Crystal thrilled at her effect on him.

He held up a flier, his nostrils flaring in a way that made Crystal a little nervous now. "This is the same as telling everybody that my father and I stole your reindeer."

"Caribou. It says right there he's a caribou, though the scientific name is the same for reindeer and caribou, Rangifer Tarandus. And you did steal him."

He looked around as if to find somebody to corroborate his lie. Oh, this is rich, she thought. He said, "You can't impugn my character over this damn reindeer."

"Watch your mouth. Kids will be showing up any minute. And you realize how pitiful you sound trying to separate yourself from your father? If he took Rudolph, you should be accepting responsibility to clear the family name."

With an about-face, and her heartbeat wildly erratic, she began marching with her fliers down the snowy sidewalk. He caught up with her inside the post office, a block away from the North Pole.

"You're not putting up these fliers," Peter said.

Crystal called out to the heavy-set woman in the blue uniform shirt. "Howdy, Rita. Got a favor to ask."

Rita Johnson, mother of Gretchen, had been Crystal's friend since high school. Her husband ran the hardware store.

Rita smiled her prettiest smile, but it wasn't for Crystal.

Peter had taken off his stocking cap and was combing his fingers through the thick chestnut hair with its tantalizing flecks of gray at the temples. Crystal noticed he hadn't shaved this morning. His rakish appearance made him downright delicious looking. To her horror, she was actively salivating. Swallowing, she whipped back to Rita.

"Don't get your hopes up, Rita. This man is a criminal. Can I put these up?"

Rita read the flier, then frowned at Peter. "You should be ashamed. Stealing Rudolph."

"I didn't," Peter said, tapping at his sheaf of fliers. "This is a misunderstanding."

Rita shook her head, tsking at the flier. "But he was kidnapped on your property. It says that right here and I know Crystal. She wouldn't lie." She came around the counter and headed for the bulletin board.

Crystal laid a sweet smile on Peter. "We could take this to court."

This time a growl came out of his throat. "You people are nuts. Worse than my father. I'll find your reindeer, but I didn't do it. I don't believe my father did it. There's something in the air around here at Christmastime. I feel like I've been trapped in another universe!"

"Oh, you have," Crystal said, relishing making the powerful man squirm. "It's called Moonstone, Wisconsin. Welcome home."

Peter marched over to stop Rita from tacking up the flier next to the FBI's "Most Wanted" list. Crystal stifled a giggle when Rita slapped his hand.

"You can't take it down," Rita said. "This is federal property. You deface federal property, I'll have you arrested."

About to burst, Crystal figured this was a good time to escape out the door.

Except that she ran into Randy Mellen, who picked her up, then dipped her. The fliers went scattering in the snow.

"How's my baby?"

"Randy?"

Still built like the jock he was in high school, he dipped her with the other arm. "Darlin', look at you. Wearin' make-up just for me. Aren't you cute as a button." He finally let her back on her feet.

She wanted to die. Peter stood with a devilish hike of an eyebrow, looking at them both.

Randy, who never wore gloves, even in the coldest weather, reached out to Peter. "Hello, there. Randy Mellen's the name, claiming her as my girlfriend is my fame."

Crystal wanted to slither over the snowbank on the street corner and hide.

Peter shook Randy's hand, all the while peering at her with penetrating eyes. "I didn't realize Crystal had a boyfriend, being the kind of woman she is."

What'd Peter mean by that? There was that urge again to kick him in the shins.

Randy chortled. "She's a sexy machine, that's the kind of woman she is for sure." Randy slapped an arm around her shoulders and jiggled her. "Hey, baby, I'm gonna have to cancel out of tonight. You okay with that?"

Peter waited too eagerly, she thought, for her answer.

Untangling herself from Randy's arms, she said, "No problem. What came up?"

Randy shrugged, then kissed her on the cheek with a smacking sound before he said, "Oh, honey, a little Christmas shopping. I got my eye on something special for ya, and I better pick it up tonight or I might be too late." He popped a quick kiss on her lips. "Tell ya what, I'll bring home a doggie bag for ya. We can have lunch together tomorrow."

"Wait. Aren't you playing Santa today?"

"Darlin', I just told ya, I got some things to do in secret." He winked, looked at his watch and said to Peter, "Nice meetin' ya."

With a wave at Peter, Randy took off down the street.

"Ahem."

"What's that supposed to mean?" Crystal began picking up fliers from the snowbank.

"You go out with a man who says he'll bring you a doggie bag from his meal?"

"Oh, he didn't mean that. Randy's cool."

"No he's not."

She looked up and noticed he'd taken that protective stance he'd shown yesterday when he thought she was a street person begging at his door. "What business is it of yours?"

"I thought maybe you'd worn make-up for me!"

Her mouth slaked dry. She became conscious of how pink and shiny her lips must be with Rose Blush Number Five. And how ridiculous her lashes must look with Black Over Black Luscious Lash.

Squaring her shoulders, she shuffled the fliers between her mittens. Then she decided the truth was the only way out of this one. "I did wear make-up for you."

"Liar."

This man was impossible. "No, actually, I did. I'm willing to use any weapon I have to negotiate the return of Rudolph. I'm assuming you have ransom demands."

"I do? Oh. Yes. Of course I do. I want something very much."

He gave her a lascivious glance from the top of her head down to her boots and back up again, where his gaze settled on her lips with Rose Blush Number Five. Her toes wiggled inside her boots. She willed them to stop. She refused to give in to this man's effect because she couldn't trust Peter LeBarron's intentions. He and his father wanted the mayor out of office, after all, which meant the LeBarrons would control Moonstone. But why go to all that trouble? What was the big secret that motivated the Rudolph scam? On one level, she agreed with Peter. None of this made sense. Everybody had gone nuts.

Picking up more of her fliers from the snow, Peter said, "Let's negotiate my ransom demands over lunch." He stepped into her air space again, their steam commingling. "I'm suddenly feeling like a bear who somebody woke up during hibernation. He's oh so hungry." He leaned close enough to absorb her reflection in his chocolate eyes.

A tremor filled her. He licked his lips. Her toes curled in betrayal. This was going all wrong. She had started the morning as the huntress, expecting to get Rudolph back from Peter by now. Somehow, she'd become the hunted.

After they separated with a promise to meet at lunchtime, Peter started back down the sidewalk toward what he knew now was the North Pole. He shook his head, letting a smile slide onto his face at the thought of his father playing Santa many years ago.

The smile soon evaporated. News spread fast in the small town. He'd become a pariah overnight. Now there were the fliers being posted everywhere.

First, Mayor Bob Winters stopped his car in the street to yell at him. "I'm not quitting. Your old goat of a father can rot in that mansion for all I care."

Now that was Christmas cheer. The mayor drove on.

Then a couple caught up with him with a little boy between them and scolded Peter for putting people out of work. They introduced themselves as the Danes, and pointed out that their boy, Marcus, had been prevented from an important childhood activity--getting his picture taken with Rudolph. Lowell Dane growled, "You're not going to scar my boy for life. None of you are. Not that teacher, not you in your fancy house. You'll hear from me."

More holiday cheer.

When Peter reached the crèche and saw the crowd of kids, his heartbeat skittered faster. The urge to run overwhelmed him. At the sight of him, two little boys, obviously twins, both pointed at him and in unison started to bawl. They cried out, "Where's Rudolph? You stole Christmas! We won't get presents!"

A woman bundled up in a camouflage snowmobile suit and red elmer cap rushed over. "This thing between you and the mayor isn't funny to children. You should be horse-whipped. But maybe some good will come of it. We can stop this ridiculous holiday display that keeps giving my husband ulcers every year."

"I'm sorry, I didn't catch your name." Peter forced himself to take off his gloves and offer her a hand.

"Mrs. Bob Winters."

The mayor's wife scoffed at the proffered hand and hurried off.

When Peter scanned the Square, he saw more people hiking toward the animals--and him. He escaped up his own sidewalk and into the mansion. But he could hear the angry babble and kids crying out near the street. What the heck had he landed in by coming to Moonstone this weekend?

"Dad," he bellowed up the staircase, "we need to talk."

At twelve-thirty Peter LeBarron found himself in the small town of Port Cliff, ten minutes from Moonstone and along the Lake Superior shoreline. From the street, the Port Cliff Casino looked like a nondescript warehouse with a glass atrium abutting the street. Peter wondered why Crystal would drag him here to negotiate the deal for Rudolph. Would they play bingo, and whoever won got the four-legged beast?

He'd never been to a Wisconsin Indian casino. He'd left the state as they started getting approval to dot the state and shake money out of the pants of retired people. Inside, the place was replete with mirrored walls, red carpeting, and murals depicting whitetail deer, beavers, wolves, and giant musky leaping from a lake.

People bundled up against the wind chill factor of minus-ten filed past him in hordes into the room with bright lights. The slot machines dinged and whirred with increasing intensity. This was obviously "the" place for lunch in little Port Cliff.

Peter guessed the buffet was somewhere beyond the gambling area. The smells of the place twisted around him like vines in a jungle ready to choke him. He'd been to jungles. He wanted to find one now and hide. His stomach churned in fear. What would he be forced to eat?

"Isn't this great?" Crystal rescued him. She came through the door with a smile, pulling off her stocking cap and shedding her coat and mittens.

A pink sweater accentuated the glow in her cheeks. She looked good enough to eat, he thought, a much better choice than the buffet somewhere in the maw of the casino.

"This is quite the place," he said. "Perfect for negotiating a reindeer."

He found the way she flipped her hair over a shoulder distracting. Did she really date that lout Randy?

"This place opened last year. It provides fifty jobs that weren't here before."

"So you brought me here to skewer me about my father selling the coal yard and letting a few people go to sweeten the deal? Perhaps they could find jobs here."

He realized his mistake the moment the words came out of his mouth. A cloud had skated over her face. "I'm sorry," he said. "That was flippant of me. I don't want anybody losing a job because of my father's inept actions."

Her sunny smile came back. "Come along. The reason we're here is that I have an errand to do, and then we can sit down to lunch."

They walked through the casino filled with mostly gray-haired patrons.

When they came to the cafeteria, decorated with stuffed animal heads on the walls, Peter saw a long line at the buffet. Happy chatter filled the room. A Native American woman in a white uniform and a scarf to keep her hair in check, walked up to them with a toothy smile.

"Miss Hagan, it's a pleasure. Pork chops and sauerkraut's the special today, but we have venison sausage pizza, too, and venison burgers. I know how you love those."

"Sounds heavenly."

Peter winced.

Crystal introduced him to Claire Lone Eagle, the mother of one of her students, Michael.

Crystal said to Claire, "After Michael found out yesterday that Rudolph hadn't come home, he seemed to have some concern about his father not coming home. Is there anything I can do to help him feel safe during school next week? I can't guarantee that I'll get Rudolph back."

Guilt burned inside Peter. While he'd been arguing with his father minutes ago about selling the household furniture, Crystal's concern was for a lonely little boy.

Claire Lone Eagle said, "With that storm, his father decided to go south with a crew. They found a construction job down in St. Louis."

"Will he be coming home for Christmas?"

Claire winced. "We need the money. Don't say anything to Michael."

Peter adjusted his stance to consider the weight of what she'd said.

A little boy with big brown eyes and a thatch of black hair come up behind his mother and hugged her legs.

"Look who's here," Claire said, her eyes sparkling. "Now don't be shy."

"Hi, Miss Hagan," Michael said. "Who's that man?"

Peter knelt down. "I'm Peter. I'm Miss Hagan's helper today. I helped her with Alice and Gracie."

Claire patted her son's shoulders. "We'll go see them later, Mike. Okay?"

Michael came out from behind his mother. "If you're a helper, are you like an elf?"

Everybody laughed.

"I'm too big to be an elf, but you could certainly be an elf. I bet Santa would love having you as a helper. I bet you help your mom all the time."

To Peter's surprise, Michael came out from behind his mother's legs and marched right up to Peter. "Can you give me a ride on your shoulders?"

Claire rushed over to take Michael's hand. "Michael. That's not polite."

An awful memory whooshed through Peter of a helicopter's machine gun strafing. He almost rushed from the casino, but then the questioning look on Crystal's face stopped him. She couldn't possibly know the secret that made his chest tighten, and neither could Michael, who looked at him with wide, brown eyes.

"Michael, why do you want me to give you a ride?"

"Because you're so tall! I could pretend I'm in an airplane. Have you been in an airplane?"

Too many times. "Lots of times."

With a glance at Claire for approval, Peter picked up Michael and settled him behind his neck. Two small hands reached around and covered Peter's eyes.

"Hey, Mr. Lone Eagle," Peter said, laughing, "airplane pilots have to see. How about you hang on here." He moved the tiny hands up to his forehead. "What's our flight plan?"

"What's a flight plan?"

Peter looked at Crystal, who still wore a confused expression. "Miss Hagan, what have your students been studying in school?"

"Christmas traditions in other lands. Mexico, Sweden, France."

"Then we're flying to France. Want to go to Paris, Michael?"

"To Paris!" the little boy crowed high in the air.

His mother laughed.

When Peter turned to Crystal, his heart almost stopped because he swore he saw a teardrop sliding down her cheek. Determined not to embarrass her, he said, "What would you like us to bring you from Paris, Miss Hagan?"

He could see her gathering herself, but before she could speak, Michael said, "Let's find Rudolph and bring him back for Miss Hagan. Okay?"

The teardrop escaping from one of Crystal's eyes gave Peter an unexpected catch in his heart. If this was how she started negotiations, Peter was in trouble.

Chapter 4

The tangy vinegar smell of the sauerkraut and pork chop special drifted on the casino cafeteria air. Crystal and Peter had found a back booth, settling into the red vinyl seats where they could hear each other over the clatter of plates and chatter about wins and losses. The money talk prompted Peter to tell animated tales about his financial services firm in Phoenix. What amazed Crystal was that as they talked Peter appeared to relish food he obviously didn't usually eat, including the pork chop and sauerkraut special, a helping of mac and cheese, tater tot casserole, and a side of green marshmallow gelatin salad.

Working on her mac and cheese, she said, "You enjoy making money for other people."

His enthusiastic nod charmed her. "It's rewarding to see somebody's nest egg grow, or see them retire as a multi-millionaire and they never expected it."

"Not too many of those around here."

"You never know. I don't judge a person's personal fortune by the cut of their clothes."

Now that surprised her, considering his background and the world in which he worked.

Peter saw the confusion on her face and said, "You thought I was all about appearances. Because I'm a LeBarron?"

"You always lived in a pretty big house, had all the best toys, and went off to a private high school and college, and then never came back."

He laid his fork down with great care, then wiped his mouth with the paper napkin and stared at her.

Crystal's insides churned. "I'm sorry," she said. "I made that all sound like an indictment. That was petty of me. I'll go get dessert. What would you like?"

As she rose, his hand snaked out to stop her. "I didn't leave Moonstone because we had money. I left because I had to. Because of the circumstances of my mother's death."

She eased back into the vinyl booth and into compassion for him. "You don't have to tell me anything. Losing a parent devastates a teenager. You had to get away."

"But you don't know the whole story. She had a drinking problem combined with depression. As a teenager, and well into my twenties, I blamed my dad for neglecting the situation for too many years."

"I'm sorry. All I ever heard was that she drowned."

"She'd been drinking and took off. The keys to the car shouldn't have been available to her. She bought a ticket on one of the dinner cruises and fell off. On purpose, I suspect. It should never have happened."

Her heart pounded for him. He worried his hands into a fist on the table. She reached out. His long fingers, warm and quaking, quieted under her touch. "You must miss your mother very much."

He took her hands in his and squeezed. A gentle warmth meandered up her arms. Then he smiled at her, which took her off-guard, and said, "She could bake the best blueberry pie."

Crystal smiled. His moroseness had passed.

"It did me good to leave Moonstone," he said, dark eyes deepening and finding the echoes of his past. "If I'd stayed I'd have been stuck working for my father and that wouldn't have worked. We would have been matches and dynamite together. I had to have space to outgrow my anger."

"Because you were robbed of all the normal things kids had, especially like now, at the holidays."

Nodding, he said, "And it seems like my father and I can't talk much at the holidays without the elephant being in the room. We try to avoid talking about her, but then one of us slips and before I know it we're in an argument. I feel like a heel, like I'm fourteen again."

He clung to her hands, his fingers massaging as he pondered. A tiny door in her heart opened so that she might invite him in for comfort.

"Hey, come on, Peter, go easy on yourself on that score. All of us bring up things that aren't resolved from our childhood. I can't forgive my mother for not letting me shave my legs until I was sixteen."

He laughed out loud, her desired result. She began giggling, too.

He let go of her hands and reached for his coffee cup. "Hairy legs. Now there's something to argue about over Christmas dinner with the family gathered."

"The problem is, my mother really does bring it up. That and the time I broke our living room window. Actually, Lucas Welch broke it. I'd thrown a rock at him, and he threw one back, which missed me but got the window. He stole my bike and tore off, leaving me to face my parents alone. The good thing that came of it was I paid for the window by helping pick strawberries on a farm and that's when I found my love for animals and growing things."

"Hmm. If my father didn't take Rudolph, it could be Lucas who took Rudolph. Back for revenge."

"Lucas? Revenge after something like thirty years?"

Peter's eyes twinkled. "Who are your enemies?"

"Enemies?"

To her chagrin, Peter took the paper placemat out from under his plate, moved the plate aside and flipped the placemat over. He took a pen from a pocket and began making a list.

"We're making an enemies list. People who could've kidnapped Rudolph. You've got the mayor."

That didn't make sense. "Why would he steal Rudolph?"

"To rile up the town, to speed the sale of the North Pole along. But then there's his wife."

"Tootsie Winters? She's harmless."

"I don't think so. She met up with me today and it was clear she'd love to be done with all this business. And there was a couple called the Danes who didn't seem to care for you."

"Their son Marcus is the school brat. He's flunking everything, gets into fights, so I call the parents into the office with the principal on a regular basis."

"Bingo," Peter said, writing down their names. "Great motive for revenge on you. Let's see, we have four on the list so far. Who else?"

Crystal looked at the eager brown eyes and cocked head across from her. The thought that Peter might be on to something settled over her. "Kirk and Jeri Kaminski."

"Who are they?" He wrote their names down.

"Mary and Joseph. Or at least they were supposed to play them in the live crèche before they demanded money."

"Motive enough. They take Rudolph until you cough up a salary for them standing in the below-zero weather for an hour for picture-takers."

"You make it sound like it's my fault that my own reindeer is missing."

She reached for her water glass while he wrote down her name on the paper!

Tapping the placement, she said, "You may as well put your own name down there."

"You're right. Silly of me. And my father's." He scratched pen to placemat. "And Leonard Moline. Wow. Look at this list of your enemies. An even ten. Who else doesn't like you? There must be more."

"More?"

Peter's broad smile sent a tickle into her middle. Or maybe it was indigestion. But her toes wiggled inside her boots. That was a bad sign. She was enjoying this man niggling her, and enjoying him too much. She had no business feeling anything for this man who would be leaving Moonstone by Sunday night. Besides, he could still have her reindeer.

She got up from the booth and grabbed her coat.

"Where are you going?" he asked.

"I've got a date to get ready for. I actually have friends."

"No. He canceled."

Dang. That's right. Being around Peter made her lose her wits. "I'm going out to hunt for Rudolph."

"Don't you need to go check on Gracie and Alice first?"

Dang again.

"I'll help," he said, getting up to trail after her through the casino.

"Gracie's missing! Where's Gracie?" The donkey was gone from the straw-filled stable. Crystal's heartbeat skittered into her throat as she looked about the crowded Square. Shoppers hurried in and out of the grocery and hardware store. Children, waiting for their parents, were playing tag in the snow in the small park in the middle of town. But there was no donkey.

Crystal looked up at Peter, who stared toward the mansion. He said, "It's got to be Leonard Moline."

"I suspected him from the first. But why? Where is he taking my animals? You said you looked all over the mansion and found no trace of them."

He kept staring at the house.

"What are you thinking?"

Peter shook his head. "My father, peering from the second-floor windows, certainly could see when nobody was around the crèche and could call an accomplice."

"I hadn't thought of that. He wouldn't be that mean, would he?"

"Manipulative, you mean." Peter gave her a meaningful glance. "He's a businessman who's always gotten his way. He obviously wants you to convince the mayor to step down."

"So we're back to square one, as they say. I've talked to Bob and that man's not budging off his mayoral butt."

Anger pushed her into action. She got Alice from the stable and Peter helped with the ramp. They loaded Alice, who nuzzled Peter in the face as she trotted into the straw-filled, enclosed trailer.

A sadness overwhelmed Crystal. "Gracie got her name from one of my students two years ago. The little girl's mother had died in an auto accident. I had just taken in the donkey from people who were moving to Superior."

"Gracie was her mom's name?"

Crystal swallowed a lump in her throat. Her eyes went blurry. "I'm taking Alice home."

"Wait." Peter grabbed her arm. "She'll be safe in there. We can keep an eye on the trailer. Why don't we look around while the trail is fresh? Somebody must've seen something. We might spot tracks, and we need to do it now before everything gets obscured. We'll find Gracie and Rudolph."

With the intensity in his dark brown eyes, she believed him.

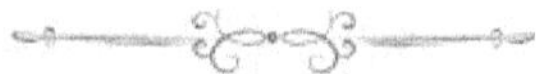

While Crystal started down the street toward the post office to question Rita, Peter decided to cross the street for the playground. He suspected a sweet teacher wouldn't motivate the kids to cough up secrets, but an intimidating stranger who lived in the notorious North Pole might.

Amid squeals, the several children chased each other through a maze of snow trails they'd created, playing a form of tag where nobody was allowed to step outside the trails.

"Hey, kids, did you see anybody take Miss Hagan's donkey?"

They stopped their play. To Peter's surprise, every rosy-cheeked face and pair of wide eyes looked guilty. A little conspiracy?

A girl in a pink, hooded coat sniffled. "Gracie's gone?"

Okay, she didn't appear guilty. "Yup," Peter said. "How long have you guys been playing here?"

A boy raised his hand as if they were in a classroom. Peter almost smiled. "Yes?"

"I've been here since my mom went into the post office."

That wasn't giving Peter much. But another boy suddenly picked up a crusty chunk of snow and sailed it past Peter's head. Peter flinched inside his coat, but hoped it didn't show.

"Nice shot. What's your name?"

"Marcus Dane."

Ah. The trouble-maker in Crystal's class. Peter had met the parents earlier. Could this kid have stolen the animals? He hadn't thought to put any kids on the list of enemies. "Well, Marcus, how long have you been hanging out here today?"

"Been here most of the day."

"Out here? In the cold?"

"No. I go inside the stores to get warm then I come back out."

"Where are your parents?"

"They went to Superior."

"They left you here?"

Marcus shrugged it off, wiping his nose with a sleeve. "I can take care of myself."

"Do they do that often?" This wasn't helping him find Rudolph or Gracie, but Peter found this boy's parents' actions disturbing.

"Sure. They said it's Christmas and they had to go shopping. They're buying me big presents. They go like every day now to buy stuff."

The little girl in pink started crying. "I won't get any presents. Rudolph doesn't like us. He ran away."

Her plea pierced his heart. Peter went over to her and kneeled down. "We're going to find Rudolph and Gracie. Let's all be detectives, okay? You can help. What's your name?"

"Gretchen."

"Gretchen, if you hear anybody talking about a reindeer and a donkey, you'd tell your parents, right?"

She nodded.

"You'd tell Miss Hagan or other people at your school, right?"

She nodded again, her tears subsiding.

"Good. You're all recruited now, okay?" He pointed back to the mansion. "I'm visiting the North Pole, and I need elves to help me find Rudolph." He got up from his crouch.

Gretchen went wide-eyed. "Are you Santa?"

Marcus piped up, "What a nerd. Of course he's not Santa."

Peter chuckled. "Hey, no name calling. It's Christmas and you may get a lump of coal in your stocking."

Gretchen wouldn't give up. "But Santa lives at the North Pole, and if that's the North Pole, then Santa must live there."

True enough. Peter smiled at her. "Gretchen, you're right. Santa used to live there. I bet if we find Rudolph and bring him back here, maybe Santa would come back for a visit to see what you want for Christmas."

Now why had he blurted that out? The kids cheered and returned to chasing about in the snow. Marcus threw one more snow clod at Peter as he turned to go. Peter noticed that neither snowball had hit him, by design, he suspected. He, too, remembered what lengths a boy would go to for a little attention from a grownup.

Feeling his fingers growing numb from the cold and wondering how little kids could be oblivious to freezing temperatures, Peter hurried to catch up with Crystal, all the while pondering the conspiratorial look he'd seen on the children's faces.

Chapter 5

Crystal's shopping basket was bulging when she saw Peter coming at her down the aisle of Johnson's Hardware Store. Her heart filled with hope at his jaunty pace.

"You found Gracie and Rudolph?"

Pulling off the black stocking cap, he said, "No. But I've got a posse working on it."

"You called the sheriff?"

"Mostly your first graders. The kids at the park."

Maybe the ruddy color in his cheeks wasn't from the cold. He was delirious with a fever. "You're sending kids out to find my animals?"

"I got to thinking. You know how gossip gallops through this place? How kids like to one-up each other by telling each other secrets? And don't kids know everything, more than parents usually do?"

She had to smile at that. "You're clever. Kids hear a lot of stuff they shouldn't. They just might hear about somebody taking a donkey or reindeer somewhere."

Taking her heavy basket, he said, "You found out nothing?"

"Rita hadn't heard anything, though she was hearing a lot of sympathy for me when patrons saw the poster. I saw Bob Winters and he's ready to call in the sheriff, but I told him to hold off a bit. I even told him his own wife might be the perpetrator."

"Oh great."

Crystal grabbed a roll of Christmas wrapping paper from a display and put it into the basket that Peter carried for her. "Don't worry. He actually thought that a possibility. Tootsie's been complaining about him working too many hours. She wants to retire and travel in the winter instead of enduring these temperatures."

"Smart woman."

Crystal noticed how easily the two of them were shopping together. Randy would never be caught shopping for anything that didn't have to do with hunting or fishing. She found it a wonder that he was shopping for her Christmas gift tonight.

When they got to the counter with the over-flowing basket, Peter asked about the odd mix of items that ranged from popcorn to colored pencils to coin purses.

"Since Randy canceled our date, I thought I might as well make my gift packages tonight for my kids instead of doing it tomorrow. Next week's our last week before vacation."

Peter's expression soured.

"What's wrong?"

"We're on the verge of figuring out what happened to Rudolph and Gracie. I thought you'd be eager to work on the case with me--your case."

The same odd feeling she'd had earlier returned, that one where she feared him invading her space but she liked free-falling into it just the same. Then she remembered that he'd be leaving tomorrow night and she'd never see him again. She realized how silly it was to worry about these feelings for Peter at all.

"You know how to make popcorn balls?"

He grinned. "No. But that sounds far more fun that spending the evening with my grumpy father and Leonard Moline. I'll bring dinner. Then you can have me do anything you want."

She gulped. Any man that handsome, even with hair mussed by a stocking cap, shouldn't say things like that.

"That's Blanca and that's Parda," Crystal said, introducing Peter to the goats in the pen in her barn.

Peter had arrived early at five-thirty. Although he'd turned up his nose at the smell of the manure she'd mucked out of the pens and into a wheelbarrow by the door, he shut the door fast and came in anyway to escape the cold. The wind howled outside, but they were toasty in the heated building filled with competing fragrances of straw and hay.

The goats bleated, climbing at the pen's gate to greet Peter. He still had on his coat, and Blanca nibbled at a sleeve.

"Hey," Peter said. "Why does every one of your animals try to eat me?" To his credit, he didn't leap back as he had earlier with Alice and Gracie, but instead reached out to scratch the goat's neck.

"I'd like to say they're acting like watch dogs to protect me, but I know better. Blanca and Parda are looking for a handout." She went to get the grain bucket off its nail hook to feed them.

"Blanca and Parda. White and brown. Were they also named by your class?"

"Yup. They're learning Spanish words. I got Blanca and Parda a month ago from a couple who moved to Minneapolis. I'm hoping to train these gals to pull a cart with my kids in it for our Memorial Day parade. The reading books I have picked out focus on animals so it should work our well."

"Everything about your life is those kids."

Something about his statement made her pause at the gate with the grain bucket and look at him pointedly. "Yeah. And I like it."

"No, I meant that they are your life. I'd think you'd have kids of your own by now."

A flush crept up her face. "Isn't that rather personal?"

Chuckling, he continued petting the goats. "I didn't really mean it to be. The way you're involved in doing things for them and caring for your animals, the question came naturally. Randy strikes me as a guy ready to make a few kids to take hunting and fishing with him."

Now her face was burning. She tried to conjure indignation, but then realized what he said troubled her for another reason. She and Randy had never talked about kids. But that wasn't Peter's business.

"You're supposed to be here to help me figure out where Rudolph and Gracie are," Crystal said, climbing the wood gate.

"That's why I'm asking about Randy."

She almost fell into the pen, but Peter caught her hips with both hands. She leaned over to pour the grain into the feed bin, giving Peter a perfect shot of her denim-clad backside, to her chagrin. The goats hopped over to munch dinner.

"Why would you think Randy might pull such a stunt?" she asked, settling into a perch atop the gate, fearful now of falling into Peter's arms.

Taking the empty bucket out of her hands, he grinned up at her. "The man's jealous!"

"Of a caribou? And a donkey?"

"Of how popular you are."

"Me?"

"You strike me as the kind of girl all the guys would have wanted on their arm at prom."

"Hah! Yeah, look at me. This was me back in those days, too. Jeans, flannel shirt, eau d'manure. No way would you have asked me to the prom."

He flinched, which surprised her. "That's what you think? That I would've skipped asking you?"

"You must have a dozen beauties back in Phoenix waiting for you to get on bended knee right now. I suspect you had your pick at your private school as well."

He flashed her a lopsided grin. "Oh yeah, I'm a catch. I rarely see the inside of my condo. When I'm not at the office I'm traveling to meet with corporate clients. Every dinner out is a working dinner."

She gave him a hard look. "You're trying to tell me you're boring? That you didn't enjoy your prom or something?"

"Oh, I can dance, if that's what you're asking."

To her shock, he toss the bucket aside, reached up to grab her, then twirled her around in the barn.

"Peter! Put me down!"

But he was laughing, twirling her into a waltz with her boots off the floor. "Ah, you prefer a two-step," he said.

He stepped to and fro up and down the narrow, straw-strewn alleyway of the barn. They were cheek to cheek, his freshly-shaved one warm against her own. She could smell the hint of soap on him. Her heartbeat thumped against his. Despite herself, she started to giggle. Being as tall as she was, no boy or man had ever held her like this--up in the air. She was flying in his arms.

Peter broke into twirling her around again, and without gravity she became giddy. Or maybe just dizzy. "Peter, stop."

He set her on her feet. She took a moment to rid herself of the slight wooziness, then peered up at him. He had a big lopsided grin on his face.

"That was fun," he said.

They were both breathing hard. The sparkle in his dark eyes scared her because it made her want to leap into his arms and ask to fly again. To escape the crazy thought, she stepped away to pick up the grain bucket he'd tossed aside. She held it in her arms like a shield against him. Her heart skittered faster at the thought of him staying for dinner.

The energy of their sudden dance followed them inside her cabin. The air crackled around them. She had an awareness of Peter that heightened her senses, drawing her to him in ways she didn't want. She didn't want to be consumed with any attraction for a man who could use her and move on. She wasn't that silly of a woman.

It didn't help that under his coat Peter wore the cream-colored cable sweater that somehow made his chestnut hair look all the richer and his eyes dark as devil's food cake. After taking off his boots by the door, he limped in thick socks, then declared, "You have a nice cabin."

She wanted to ask about the limp, and ask about how he managed to twirl her so well in the barn with a leg that bothered him, but thought better of encouraging more personal questions. She went to the open kitchen area to get out plates and silverware. She smelled roast chicken in the bag he'd brought.

"It's an old logger's cabin," she told him. "Those are the original logs from when it was built in the 1920s. I've been adding on the other rooms."

"By yourself?" He placed a broad palm on a log in a way that made her remember the warmth in those hands at lunchtime and their firmness on her hips when he'd steadied her in the barn and helped her fly through the air. The cabin grew warmer.

She dug into the bag to bring out the contents wrapped in heavy aluminum foil. "I hire high school kids for heavy lifting. I added the room for my office last summer. Otherwise you'd have been met with stacks of papers and junk in here."

"So we've got plenty of room for making those popcorn balls and gift packages."

When she looked up from the table, he was taking off his sweater. His action lifted up the shirt and t-shirt underneath the sweater by accident to reveal lean stomach muscles. She almost dropped the plate in her hands. A tanned six-pack was an *hors d'oeuvre* she hadn't expected him to bring with dinner. The tickle in her toes zipped up through her body where the feeling settled low in her midsection.

As he wrestled the sweater off and tucked in a red-and-black checked flannel shirt, she averted her gaze to the task of setting out dinner.

Rolling up his sleeves, he approached the table, the slight limp putting a swagger in his gait that made Crystal focus shaky fingers on unwrapping the foil around a bowl of garlic mashed potatoes. "Let's eat," she said. "I'm famished."

The food wasn't enough of a distraction. His tales of his travels to South America mesmerized her. As Peter unleashed his enthusiasm for adventure, she saw an entirely different man than the one she'd met last night. She found herself asking questions and prompting him so that she could continue enjoying herself. She imagined riding in the dugout boat with him, hitting rapids in rivers filled with snakes. Peter's stories certainly put to shame Randy's fishing excursions to Canada with buddies.

Before she knew it, she and Peter had finished dinner and were elbow deep in popcorn and sticky syrup, engaged in easy chatter about everything from the weather in Phoenix and the Amazon, to his tales of woe about the stock market. An hour later, with twenty-six popcorn balls--two for each student--sat in lines on wax paper, Peter mentioned it was time to leave. Crystal realized in a panic they hadn't even begun talking about a new plan to find Rudolph and Gracie. But most importantly, she didn't want Peter to leave. The yearning defied common sense. She knew the danger in it.

"Stay for coffee. You need fortification before going out there. It'll give us time to go over your list and check it twice."

Their gazes collided across the table, then dipped away. His red-checked shirt lured her thoughts. What would it be like to be held in the folds of those arms and that soft, flannel shirt, nestled against him during the cold night, smelling the hint of the hay and straw in the barn on him yet, as she let their lips...

What the heck was she thinking! She had a boyfriend!

"You know," she said, kicking back her chair, "it might be best if you go. I'm tired. All the stress, I'm sure. You understand?"

"Of course," Peter said, waving his sticky hands. "I'll wash up, then help you wrap the popcorn balls so we can go to bed faster."

Her heart flip-flopped at the double meaning. She guessed by now he loved to tease her, so she hurried behind him to the sink, where she turned on hot water.

Rubbing elbows with him, however, at the sink was a mistake. His breath feathered the hair at her temple. With trembling, sticky hands, she poured liquid soap on his hands and he began lathering up. When she dumped the bottle upside down to squirt soap on her own, he took her hands in his and set the bottle aside.

"I've got too much," he said, "let's share."

He began massaging her hands in his warm, foamy ones, taking her breath away again. When he immersed their hands under the water, working magic with his fingers to loosen the sticky goo from the two of them, her heart wanted to stop. He rubbed each finger, working with gentle pressure up and down. The slosh of the water took on a rhythm suggestive of actions more primal. Her cheeks burned.

When his lips touched her temple, she thought at first it was only his breath again.

But then one of his hands lifted from the hot water to cup her chin. His thumb left its warm, wet imprint on her lower lip. Dipping his head, he nibbled at the drip of water, following another droplet as it eddied down her chin, catching it as it slid along her throat.

Crystal imagined coursing down the Amazon with him, heat shimmering between them.

Then the window rattled with the wind and a chill whipped between them.

Peter had stepped back. "I'm sorry. I was way out of line."

The chill was real. Peter rushed to put on his sweater and coat. To her horror, he was flustered, embarrassed even. And he was rushing away. Because she'd let him kiss her.

Before he dove out the door, she caught his coat sleeve. "Peter, it's okay. It was just a kiss. We got carried away, is all."

"No. I got carried away with another man's woman. This won't happen again."

Then he was gone into the frigid night. Her stomach clenched. She watched out a window as the red taillights of his rental car disappeared down the road to Moonstone.

Emptiness, no, *anger,* surged through her. She let the kiss happen. It wasn't Peter's fault at all. For Peter, the night had been an entertaining diversion, but she was making more of it. How foolish of her. Peter had no intention of making a life in Moonstone. His flight left for Phoenix tomorrow night.

She spotted Peter's stocking cap left behind on the chair near the door. Reaching for it, she did another foolish thing. She smelled the wool cap. Peter's essence filled her lungs. It scared her how much she longed to hear more of his stories about the Amazon.

When Peter stepped inside the mansion later that evening, his gaze swept about the pristine and austere front reception hall. He felt as hollow as the cavernous space. The only smell was the vague hint of lemon cleaner Leonard used. The only sound was the grandfather clock. Nothing made him feel needed or wanted. Peter realized he could walk through this house and through Moonstone and never leave a proverbial footprint that mattered to anybody. Yet, Crystal Hagan mattered. He wanted what she had in life. She was needed and wanted by children, goats, and Rudolph. What a fool he'd been to think he could grab a little of what she had by stealing a kiss. He'd had the strangest feeling in the cabin that by being close to her he'd somehow become a better person, as if one person could take on the best traits of another person by touching their skin.

He shook off the thoughts, hung up his coat, took off the heavy boots he still wasn't quite used to wearing and went upstairs.

Intending to head straight for his suite, he paused instead at the door of his father's dining parlor when he saw the white-haired man sitting in front of the crackling fireplace.

"Dad? It's after ten o'clock. Isn't it way past your bedtime?" His father usually folded by eight-thirty on their weekends together.

"I've been waiting up for you," Henri said, dipping a spoon into a dessert dish. "You went off to that prep school and I never got to wait up for you when you went on dates. You dated, right?"

Stunned by his father's odd question, and thinking about his prom talk with Crystal, Peter sat down in the companion chair in front of the fireplace. He hoped the blast of heat would be a good excuse for the blush crawling up his face.

"Yeah, I dated."

"How was tonight's date?"

We danced and I even forgot about my bum leg. Peter looked more closely at what his father was eating. "Chocolate pudding cake?"

"It wouldn't be such a bad idea to marry the gal just for this cake."

That made Peter smile, despite the impossibility of the notion. "She does know her way around a kitchen. And a barn. And school and kids."

"She's handy."

"I don't really want to talk about Crystal Hagan."

"Well, I do, son. Go nuke yourself a dish of this and sit with me. Help me write my obituary."

Peter's heart almost stopped. "Dad? You all right?"

"I have to do something with my spare time. Might as well use my last years writing fiction that you can print in the paper when I'm gone."

Peter watched his dad's quivering hand scoop up the chocolate sauce. They weren't fighting, which felt strange. The evening was getting weirder, but Peter decided to get some cake.

When he sat down again with his father, the steamy chocolate pudding cake made his mouth water. He scooped up a spoon, dipping it into the whipped cream on top, and savored a mouthful. His father's spoon clinked against his plate, too. They watched the fire for a moment.

Henri said, "I missed out on your prom, your dates, teaching you to drive."

Peter's nerves went on alert. This sounded like the prelude to a fight. "Dad, it's okay. That was long ago. I'm a grown man. I survived. Those things aren't a big deal anyway."

"I should've stood up for things back then."

Peter put down his spoon. "You mean, stood up against me? I was a rotten teenager with a mouth on me. But that's the past. I'm here now, and tomorrow you and I will work on the details of selling the house. I'll also take a look at the papers on the coal yard sale, if you like." Peter didn't even know himself anymore. Maybe it was the chocolate pudding cake, or the warm fire, or his father's calm mood, but Peter sensed something--someone--was causing a change within himself. He couldn't quite admit it out loud yet, but he had missed having his dad teach him how to drive and help him pick out the tux for his high school prom. A flicker of the ancient loneliness wrenched a shiver from his shoulders and made him think about Crystal again.

"Guess what I did on my so-called date tonight."

Henri set his dish on the small table between them. "You kissed her?"

Peter's ears burned. Oddly enough, he didn't mind. "Yeah, I kissed her."

"Was it good?"

"Dad?!"

"Like I said, I'm making up for lost time. What else happened?"

"Not what you're thinking." *I wanted it to go that far.* Peter escaped into a bite of the pudding cake. "I fed goats and the alpaca. I even shook out straw for their beds. And we made popcorn balls for her class."

"With red and green food dye?"

"No, we made plain balls."

"I like those things. My teeth can't handle them anymore, but I like them. You bring any home with you?"

"Now why would I do that if you can't eat them?"

"Your mother used to make them."

Peter almost dropped his plate. He focused on the fireplace, watching it dance in orange, red, and blue. The crackling reminding him of popping corn earlier at Crystal's cabin, of kissing her and tasting the sweetness of her skin. "I don't remember that about mom."

When his father didn't reply, Peter offered, "Maybe I don't remember a lot of things about her because I was trying so hard to be mad at you and the world." He remembered lunch with Crystal. "I remember Mom made a great blueberry pie."

"We used to pick the blueberries ourselves when we were first married. She loved the outdoors and gardening. Remember all her flowers?"

Regret sank deeper within Peter. "Sort of. I suppose."

"That's okay. You were just a tyke when she turned the backyard into flower gardens that ran from the house all the way to the lake. The mayor's plan would plant condos right where the annual beds used to be."

Sadness for his mother compelled Peter to go to the window. He pulled aside the heavy drapes. There was just enough moonlight for Peter to see the forty yards or so to the lake. Because of the snow, there was no discernible line where the land met Lake Superior. The white moonscape went on forever.

Henri coughed. "Some nights I've seen the Northern Lights."

Peter had never seen them. He squinted. Nothing happened. He let the drapery drop and then he sat down again.

"Before the bad times came for her, your mother held the biggest parties in town."

"I do remember some of those, even a birthday party where all the kids came and we played baseball. Mom was the pitcher." Peter grinned at the memory.

"You think that Crystal Hagan could be a pitcher to a bunch of kids?"

"Dad, she's taken. Let's not talk about Crystal. Besides, I don't think she really wants to be all that chummy with you and me unless we can somehow find her reindeer before Christmas."

"Caribou."

Peter glanced at his grinning father, who said, "Leonard picked up one of the fliers. Rangifer tarandus. They can run up to fifty miles an hour. Rudolph could be in the Dakotas by now."

"And how do you know all that?"

"Leonard has a computer in his study downstairs. I know my way around the Internet. We googled Rudolph. You ever google?"

Never mind that. He'd gone downstairs? His father had navigated the stairs somehow. Could he walk more than he was letting on to his son? A flare of the old anger with his father erupted, but Peter tamped it down. It had become impossible this weekend to hold onto old grudges after becoming involved with the hunt for a missing reindeer. Why did it take a man fifty-one years to realize the order of importance of things in life? Maybe midlife was really all about beginning life. Peter had spent fifty years learning to breathe and now he was one year old again, ready to learn to walk through life for real.

"It's great that you use the computer, Dad. I advise a lot of people over sixty about retirement finances and you'd be surprised at how many still seem scared of a computer and e-mail."

"Tell them your father's eighty-four and yahooing. That's free e-mail, you know."

Peter found all of this astounding and amusing. "What's your address?"

"North Pole at a dot com."

Peter grinned. "So there's still some Santa in you."

"It was the best job I ever had and it paid me nothing."

"But the smiles of worshipping kids in Moonstone, I bet."

"Those were the good ol' days. Nowadays they're all brats. They'd just throw snowballs at me."

Peter thought about his request of the kids and about Marcus Dane. "Who do you think might have taken Rudolph?" He poked about in a denim pocket and came up with the placemat with the enemies list. He reviewed what he and Crystal had put together.

Henri looked at the list between trembling hands. "You two should run a detective agency. Any of these people and kids could've pulled off the stunt."

"But nobody saw Rudolph or Gracie disappear and they were in plain sight."

Henri nodded, folding the paper. "Let me think on it."

"It's somebody who wants to get you and the mayor riled up. That live Nativity has been something of an institution for years, and Crystal Hagan is committed to it."

"Why don't you bring that gal around for a talk?"

"Why? What good would that do?"

"Because I think you're both thinking of this Rudolph thing too globally. You know, for a smart person you're not very smart."

"What do you mean?" Peter was genuinely intrigued and not offended.

"All these people on this list probably have a bit of a grudge against Miss Hagan. When we figure out who's the most capable of stealing live animals, and who needs them the most to destroy your Miss Hagan, we'll have our culprit."

Your Miss Hagan. Somehow the choice of words endeared his father to Peter. Peter had thought about a possible grudge against Crystal, too, and he didn't like the idea. "I don't know, Dad, she's so nice. Who'd want to harm her?"

"Maybe you need to stick around and protect her."

For a fleeting moment, the image of duking it out with Randy to protect her gave Peter a reason to grin. He shook his head. "You're not going to succeed at this matchmaking because she has a boyfriend already."

"Randall? That dentist?"

"What's wrong with a dentist?"

"Crystal Hagan can do better."

"Well then, maybe you should marry her."

"I just might. You watch out." The older man waved a hand about. "All of this would end up hers. Plus I'd get my cake on a more regular basis."

When Peter got up to go to bed, his father asked, "What would be in your obituary if you went today?"

"I don't know. Why?"

"Because I don't know! Son, I don't know you very well. Not as a grown man anyway. What makes you proud? What makes you get up in the mornings?"

Peter didn't have the kind of answers for which his father was digging. He went to bed unable to settle into sleep because of his father's words. *Crystal Hagan can do better.* But was Peter LeBarron worthy of her? *What makes you proud?*

Chapter 6

On Sunday morning the frigid temperatures broke, and with the sun out, the thermometer on the side of the barn zoomed all the way to ten above zero. Crystal had just finished the morning chores and was back in the house around nine-thirty when the phone rang. She smiled, hoping it was Peter asking to come out to retrieve the stocking cap he'd left last night.

Instead, Mayor Bob Winter's loud honking voice bowled her over. "Get to town right now! Crystal? You hear me? We've got an emergency on our hands and it's your fault and only you can fix it."

What in the world? "Bob, what happened? Did something happen at the school? Did the pipes freeze and break again and flood the library?"

"Haven't you read the Sunday paper?"

"No, it's still in my mailbox."

"You're front-page news in the *Leader-Telegram*. The headline's 'Rudolph Kidnapped in Moonstone. Will Christmas Get Canceled?' The subhead says, 'Teacher's Holiday Gift to Children in Need of Your Help.'"

Crystal sat down at her kitchen table. "Boy, news does travel fast around here. But I don't see the crisis, Bob."

"Then listen."

She heard honking horns and people talking in the background.

Bob came on the line again and said, "I'm standing in the middle of Moonstone with my cell phone because somebody has to direct traffic. People are driving in from all over to meet you and your animals. So get down here with them and bring a bucket."

"A bucket? What for?"

"For the donations. Everybody wants to know where to put the money for you to get a new Rudolph so we can have Christmas for the children."

Within an hour, Crystal was able to load Alice, Blanca, and Parda. She called the Garcia twins' father to borrow the cow the twins had trained for 4-H. Gretchen's cousin only a mile down the road let her borrow his Shetland pony, Zip. Crystal brought along a pair of fake antlers out of her closet grab bag of holiday school supplies and found her way into a Moonstone she didn't recognize.

Families and couples packed the little town. With no stoplights, the traffic poked along and drivers parked at odd angles around the tall snowbanks. Shoppers clogged the sidewalks, but she saw smiles on the faces. Rita was outside the post office with what appeared to be a makeshift and very popular hot chocolate stand.

With the mayor's help, Crystal navigated her rig through the streets to the three-sided stable. Peter was waiting for her. She handed him his stocking cap.

"Thanks." He flipped back the hood on his coat and pulled the cap down to his eyebrows. With ruddy cheeks above the hint of dimples, he looked almost jolly. She noticed he'd finally found lined mittens to wear. Mittens were much warmer than gloves in this weather. "This is insane," he said, "but in a good way, like a movie premiere and you're the star."

People crowded around them, snapping pictures of Crystal. A few in the crowd had picture phones and were talking loudly to friends and relatives. Crystal almost couldn't breathe because of the cloud of steam floating about her.

Like a pro, Peter ordered the crowd to back up a little. Then he helped her bring down the ramp and unload the animals. When he saw the cow, he asked, "A new addition?"

"Yeah, that's Crystal." When he cocked his head at her, she laughed. "The Garcia twins named her. What can I say?"

"That you're popular! I'm jealous. I've never had a cow named after me."

"That'd have to be a bull." Ach, he'd sucked her right into that sexy talk he loved.

"A bull named Peter the Great. I like it."

His laughter made the winter sunlight almost warm. She had the greatest urge to kiss him right there on the street, but the holiday crowd demanded they hurry with the animals.

As the morning's hours ticked by, Crystal must have talked with a hundred strangers who brought donations while Peter helped families with little kids who wanted their pictures taken with Zip the pony, Crystal the cow, Blanca and Parda, and Alice. When a Santa showed up to pose, Crystal asked Peter who it was. Could it be his father?

Peter, catching his breath after lifting maybe the fiftieth child off the pony, said, "It's Lowell Dane."

"Marcus's father? Helping me?"

"He said he was on his way into Duluth for a gig later and he got caught in the traffic here so he offered to help."

"Have you been watching the donation kettle?"

"He seems trustworthy. I don't think he'd pull anything on you," Peter said, his mitten-covered hand chucking her chin. "Besides, he's got a Santa suit on. He's on his best behavior."

By three in the afternoon, with the sun dipping low to the west, Crystal was exhausted. Thank goodness Peter pitched in with the mob. Tourists and shoppers still streamed by and traveled in and out of the shops, even the hardware store. They came out with bulging bags. Crystal couldn't deny the happy mood everybody was in.

Neither could the mayor. Bob Winters, wearing a Santa hat with the price tag still on from the hardware store, made his way through the street to the stable.

"You're coming back tomorrow, right?"

"Bob, I teach on Monday."

"You can't. A reporter was here. They're doing another piece on the reaction to Rudolph's kidnapping tomorrow. This is a boon for our town. Do you know how much the businesses are racking up in sales today? We want that to continue all this coming week and Christmas week. You have to bring in your animals every day."

"I can't. I borrowed the pony and the cow. And I teach. Bob, I can't do a live animal display for you. We've never done this every day. It's hard work. This has always been a one-day special thing for Moonstone."

Peter interjected himself between them. "I've got an idea. What if your kids put together an art project that happens to be cardboard replicas of all these animals? That might be a story that could charm the tourists. The kids could even do homework on the animals and come out here and talk to the tourists a little."

Crystal looked at him slack-jawed. "When are the kids supposed to do this?"

Bob hooted. "I love it. Splendid idea."

Peter said, "How about tonight?"

"The school's closed," she reminded him.

"Bring them to the North Pole."

"Your father doesn't want a house full of kids."

"You told me he used to play Santa Claus. It might do him good to have kids around."

Her heartbeat shifted into a higher gear. "You have a plane to catch."

"I'll postpone it."

Her toes wiggled inside her boots. "Do you even know what you're asking? Inviting thirteen first-graders into your house with scissors and paste and paint?"

"Leonard needs more to do anyway. He'll have it cleaned up in no time."

Bob patted each of them on the shoulders. "Perfect. Moonstone is rockin' because of you two. Now I've got to run before my wife divorces me."

Crystal didn't recognize the smiling man blinking big chocolate-colored eyes at her. A lump crawled into her throat. "You're really staying?"

"At least tonight. Seems I volunteered to herd first-graders. What do they like? Should I pick up pizzas?"

"They'll love it." Then a practical thought came to her. "Oh my gosh, I have to call all the parents and get their permissions and--"

Peter grabbed her. Feathering frost on the air, he said, "Go home now, make your calls. I'll take care of the animals and the donation pail for you."

"You must be frozen by now."

"Can't tell. I'm too numb. Now go. I'll be fine."

She wanted to kiss him again, but she didn't dare, not with all the cameras and people still mingling nearby. All the way home in her truck, she wondered why Peter stepped up for this task. The man wasn't used to kids. She wondered what disasters awaited them now.

Her worries were allayed somewhat when she discovered Marcus Dane couldn't come. His parents weren't home and therefore he couldn't get permission to come.

She told him on the phone, "It's too cold to sneak out on your bike. And don't even think about coming with a slip of paper with a fake signature, Marcus. That didn't work last time."

After changing clothes--into a sloppy sweatshirt and jeans that could withstand paste, glue, paints, and colored markers--Crystal retrieved her animals from town, did her chores, and returned to the North Pole by five-thirty.

When she walked into the mansion, effused with pepperoni pizza smells, the front hall was a sea of cardboard, one-by-two strips of wood, paint cans, and wiggle-worm children.

And Marcus Dane grinned up at her, just as he applied a dripping, red paintbrush to the back of Peter's denim jeans.

Little Michael Lone Tree saw Marcus's trickery and tackled him. Then the Garcia twins pounced and a free-for-all erupted.

Crystal yelled, "Stop that. All of you. I'm ashamed of you."

Peter plucked Marcus up first, and to her surprise, heaved Marcus up over Peter's head and onto his shoulders.

Michael pouted. "Hey, I want a ride."

Peter surveyed the twelve imps on the floor staring at him and said, "Everybody gets a ride."

Squeals of delight echoed in the cavernous hall.

"If they behave. And work hard. Elves work hard. We want to be done in an hour before your parents come for you."

Crystal had rarely seen such industriousness in her students. "Elves?" she asked Peter.

Marcus answered from his perch. "I like being an elf. I'm the head elf."

Crystal cocked an eyebrow at Peter. "You made him the head elf?"

Peter smiled. "Time for a ride." He took off for a tour of the mansion with his uneven gait, with Marcus rocking on his shoulders. She took over guiding the painting and building of a reindeer, a cow, a sheep, and a donkey.

Pizza got eaten in between shoulder rides. Thank goodness the paint was nontoxic. A good share of finger licking went on without too much hand washing in between painting stints. Crystal couldn't help but smile at Peter's easy give-and-take with the children. Looking about at the cheery art class on a Sunday night, she had to admire his idea. He was definitely teacher material.

Gretchen raised her hand between pizza bites. "Miss Hagan? Rudolph doesn't have a nose that glows."

"He's cardboard so that's okay."

Peter held up his hand. "Miss Hagan, I have the perfect solution."

He left the foyer and returned soon with what looked like an antique bedside accent lamp with a ruby glass globe. "We'll use this."

"It'll get broken," Crystal said. "It must be worth a fortune."

Peter shrugged. "If the house goes, we have to sell this anyway. Might as well turn it into a glowing nose. I can string extension cord out to the stable."

The children clapped. They thought that was the coolest idea. Crystal was outvoted.

After the parents had picked up everybody, only Marcus was left. He sat in the middle of the floor among the artistic creations laid out to finish drying. Crystal couldn't get an answer at the Dane house. She supposed Marcus's father was still doing his Santa stint at the mall in Duluth.

Peter said, "I'll take you home."

"I'd rather stay here," Marcus said. "I want another ride on your shoulders."

Crystal cringed. She knew when Marcus was about to cause a fit. His face glowed almost as red as the glass globe now fashioned on the fake Rudolph propped against a wall. "Marcus, you have to go home."

"No! I want a ride. Now."

She gasped when Marcus kicked at a can of paint, and it splattered blue up the side of the mansion wall, almost hitting the portrait of Henri.

Peter grabbed the boy before Crystal could explode like the paint can at the boy. "Come over here. Want to know why I can't give you another ride? Want to share a secret that none of the other kids know?"

Marcus nodded with wonder on his face. Peter sat down in a chair, then pulled up a pants leg, tugging it up over his knee. He proceeded to pop off his leg!

Crystal took a step back in shock, while Marcus took hold of the prosthesis and said, "Wow, cool."

"That's why I can't give you another ride. My stump's a bit sore after all the rides."

When Crystal exchanged a glance with Peter, she saw a twinge of something on his face. Embarrassment? Maybe he saw that reflected on her face. She felt horrible and stepped forward.

"When did that happen? How did it happen?" she asked.

Marcus asked, "Where did your real leg go?"

"Marcus!" Crystal admonished him.

Peter put the prosthesis back in place then rolled the pants leg down to the sock on the fake foot. "That's a good question, Marcus. I was in the Army many years ago. I left my leg back in a place where there were land mines in a field near a school. I was there to help make sure this didn't happen to a bunch of boys like you. I found the land mine, just not in the way I'd expected."

Crystal's heart ached for what Peter must have been through, and she thought Marcus felt the same sympathy, surprising her. The boy sat on the floor next to Peter's fake foot, touching it with care. "Can I stay? My mom lets me do sleepovers all the time."

Crystal expected confusion on Peter's face, but instead suspicion marked it.

Peter asked Marcus, "Why do you want to stay here?"

Marcus didn't answer. He lowered his head. Crystal had never witnessed a subdued Marcus. When she was about to go to him and pick him up from the floor, Peter shooed her away with a hand and instead eased off his chair and sat down cross-legged in front of Marcus.

Peter asked, "Is everything okay at home?"

Marcus shrugged. Crystal became concerned and sat down on the chair next to them. "Marcus, please tell us what's going on. I promise not to take you to the principal's office or anything. I won't yell at you."

When Marcus's chin tipped almost to his chest, Peter said to the boy, "I'm really proud of you tonight. Even though you painted my butt red and kicked the paint can."

It was meant to get a reaction from Marcus, but the boy only shrugged again.

"Do you know why I'm proud of you?" he asked. "Because you're a strong guy. You walked all the way over to my house alone just to make a new Rudolph for others to enjoy. Why don't I take you home? I'll wait with you until your father gets home, okay?"

Marcus kept his head down the whole time Peter helped him up and into his coat. After he'd sent him out the door to get into the car, Peter whispered to Crystal, "I think I'm about to find out who stole Rudolph and Gracie. You might want to follow me in your truck."

The sheriff arrested Marcus's father, Lowell Dane, that night at a strip mall in Duluth where Lowell thought he could make money with his own version of a live animal display. The sheriff told Crystal on the phone that Rudolph and Gracie were in good health and sharing a pen at the local animal shelter and could be picked up anytime.

Crystal and Peter had waited at the Dane house with Marcus until his mother got home. Both mother and child were mortified. Later, out in the driveway under the stars, ready to get in their vehicles and drive their separate ways, Crystal thanked Peter for his gentleness with Marcus.

"He's usually a brat. How did you guess that it was his father who kidnapped Rudolph?"

"Marcus told me about being alone in town, then he tossed some snowballs at me. Boys act out when they're covering up pain or embarrassment. I know. And I noticed how involved Lowell Dane was today in helping us out. But it dawned on me that he was looking over the animals. I saw him a couple of times patting them, as if getting them used to him."

"Why hadn't I noticed that?" She felt stupid now for not catching on.

"You were busy. And who would've thought a Santa would steal animals? It's likely why nobody noticed him taking Rudolph. Nobody would think to blame Santa. Witnesses likely assumed he was helping you. Because nobody knew Lowell was playing Santa until today, he wasn't a real suspect."

Crystal shivered, stamping her feet against the cold snow in the Dane driveway. "So he probably drove up when there weren't many around to see him anyway, nobody paid attention, and he nabbed Rudolph and Gracie."

On impulse, she stepped over and planted a kiss on his cold cheek.

"What's that for?" he asked.

Steam trailed from their nostrils. This time, she didn't back away. "You were right. The kids would give up the secret."

"Well, not until I gave up mine." He tapped his leg that wore the prosthesis. "I suspected that Marcus knew who it was. That kind of kid is a know-it-all. I have to admit, though, I'm sorry it was his own dad. The kid needs a break."

She warmed to his insight. "I agree. I'm going to go out of my way to be kind to him. He's always been the bully, but now he's probably feeling a lot of shame. Poor kid. We all want to be proud of our dads."

"I can relate."

"Thank your dad for putting up with the noise." She wanted to hug Peter, yet the realization that they weren't meant to be brought a stiffness to her limbs. "You must be exhausted, after putting up with them all day and half the night. And your leg..."

"I'll be okay." He draped an arm around her shoulder to walk her to her truck. A welcomed warmth eased the awkwardness plaguing her. "I could never do what you do. In a classroom every day all day with that crew? Not me."

She thought about his comments yesterday concerning having children. "You'd make a good dad, you know. And a good teacher. Maybe you should try that when you get back to Phoenix. Volunteer. Tell your stories."

"Maybe."

"You don't sound enthused about any of that."

When he opened her truck door, she saw the old Peter, the man who'd been upset with her when they met on Friday night. Gone was the relaxed, happy face of the past two days.

With his gaze cast down like Marcus's earlier, he said, "Why don't you give Randy a chance? He went shopping for you last night. The guy looked eager as hell. And you're not too old to have children."

"I'm old."

"No, I'm old."

"Want me to kick you in the shins?"

At least that got him to look up and grin a little. "Climb in before we both freeze our toes off."

She did. The truck started with a wheeze and a groan. She flung the heater on, then rolled down the window. Was this goodbye? Had they come to this? Strangers again?

"Well, goodbye," she said, her shoulders quaking, "and thanks. You'll help put up the display tomorrow before you leave?"

"Sure." She hit the window switch but he plunked a hand on the glass. "Wait."

He leaned in through the window, turning her face toward him with a mitten. He kissed her thoroughly, his breath steaming about her face. He tasted and smelled of pizza yet. She held onto the steering wheel, because if she didn't, her whole body would rise off the seat, drift through the window, and ask him to dance right there in the snow.

Freezing air swept over her damp lips when he backed away.

"See you tomorrow," was all he said as he disappeared into the night.

Damn the man. Crystal shoved tears off her face during the drive home. She needed windshield wipers for her eyes. She could barely see.

The longer she drove, and the closer she got to her cabin, the less she wanted to be there. She knew she'd never sleep. When she pulled into her yard, she kept the truck running, took out her cell phone and called the sheriff's department. Yes, they could have somebody go over to the Humane Society yet tonight to let her pick up Rudolph and Gracie, if she hurried. The truck clock read nine-thirty. She hitched up the trailer and took off.

But she wasn't only going to fetch the reindeer and donkey. She had an urgent need to see Randy. Maybe Peter was right. These feelings of contentment around Peter were only the stirrings of an imagined affair. She was lonely. Randy would set her straight. Randy was real. He didn't make her conjure up hot sex in her bed. What was she thinking, anyway, of wanting Peter's six-pack working on her under the sheets? After all, she was a teacher who had to be a role model for her kids. Her heart betrayed her though, skipping a beat when she recalled Peter taking off his fake leg to show Marcus. Peter understood Marcus completely. Peter was meant to have kids, despite himself.

Crystal and Randy had never talked about kids. But Randy would make a good father, too. She'd never told Randy that. Painful confusion swirled inside her. Seeing Randy tonight was a good thing. She needed to get back to reality.

She found his street in Superior and a spot between snowbanks big enough to park the truck and trailer.

She rang the bell to his ranch house, but he didn't come to the door. A light glowed inside behind the curtains, though, so she knew he must be around. She knocked. Sighing, she decided to use the key he'd given her and go in and at least leave him a note.

Once inside, she almost fainted. Then anger curdled her insides. Randy and a woman stood with only a sheet covering them. Crystal had caught them in the act trying to sneak back to the bedroom quick when they heard the front door open.

"Randy?" A part of her died inside. And it wanted to come up and spew over the floor. She clamped a hand over her mouth.

The woman hurried down the hall to the bedroom. Randy had the audacity to smile. "Hi, cupcake."

"Is this how you go shopping for Christmas? Personal service?" She wanted to kick him somewhere and it wasn't in the shins.

"Come on, hon, I just hired her. It's nothing."

"Oh, so it's an employment interview. You bastard."

Crystal choked back a sob and marched out the door, banging it behind her for good measure.

Now she understood about the broken dates, the two-timing creep. She stomped hard all the way to the truck, imagining trampling Randy's face with her boots.

Minutes later, she was never so glad to see two animals in her life. Rudolph hopped up and down off his hooves and looked like he really could fly when he saw her. Gracie brayed, almost honking at her. Crystal hugged them each fiercely after loading them in her trailer filled with extra straw and hay to comfort them. "I've got you two, and that's all I need. Men are way too much trouble."

Chapter 7

Whe she arrived at the Nativity site the next day on her way to school, the new cardboard display was already in place, replete with the many cardboard animals painted in uneven strokes of colors that made for a few surprises. Whoever heard of purple sheep? She couldn't wait to collect her students later in the day and have them come over as a group. The mayor had agreed to a little ceremony for them at two-thirty, when school let out for the day.

"Besides," Bob noted that morning, "that's when I invited the reporters to take pictures. We could probably turn this into a holiday card or calendar and sell those and use the cash to pay the health insurance for some of the folks laid off by Henri LeBarron's sale of the coal yard."

The sting of reality that Monday didn't get any better as the day wore on. Peter had caught an early flight. She doubted she'd ever see him again.

The kids seemed to sense it, too. They were as subdued as she. Michael cried because he missed both his father and the "airplane man", as he called Peter.

Marcus didn't come to school on Monday. Crystal understood it would be hard for him to face his classmates. She'd give him a couple of days, then she'd work with his mother and the school's assigned social worker to make sure Marcus got through the trauma of his father kidnapping Rudolph. She had to admit, she missed Marcus's mischief. Without him at school, the class was too quiet. She had nothing to do. Nobody to take to the principal's office. Nobody to worry about.

That night, while reviewing lesson plans for the next day, a knock came at her cabin door. When she opened it, amid a blowing snow, she gasped at the sight of an old man with white hair and using a walker. Then a smile curled his lips in a way that she recognized.

"Henri? Henri LeBarron? My gosh, get in here." She looked past him to see if Peter had brought him.

"He's not with me," Henri said, reading her mind. He hobbled in, pushing the walker ahead of him.

"You drove out here?"

"I didn't fly. You're the one with Rudolph. I, unfortunately, have only Leonard Moline."

She felt like she was back in first grade and being chided. "Sit down. Peter's all right? Where's Leonard?"

"My son is a knothead, and Leonard's fine in the car."

She was secretly glad of that. She shivered at the thought of the mysterious Leonard in her cabin.

Henri hobbled over to a comfortable chair near her fireplace. "It's too damn cold around here, you know that?"

"You could go live with Peter in Phoenix. What would you like? Some coffee?"

"Got any chocolate pudding cake?"

A smile wiggled across her lips. "No, but I could make hot cocoa."

"That's the ticket."

Why was he here? she wondered, as she poured milk into a pan with sugar and cocoa powder.

"Oh good," he said, coughing, "you make it the old-fashioned way. Want to marry me?"

She looked up. Then relaxed. He was kidding. Now she knew where Peter got his flirtatious bent with words. "Sure. Want to turn that mansion into a stable? You'd have to put up with a noisy donkey and some goats that will nibble on the banisters."

While the cocoa heated on the stove, she joined Henri, sitting across from him on a corner of the hearth. Heat from the flickering flames tickled the side of her face. "So why are you here? On a night like this? It's dangerous on the roads."

"I'm checking you out. What do you think I'm doing out here in this damn snow storm?"

Shaking her head to get rid of the fuzzy confusion, she asked again, "I must have heard you wrong. You're checking me out? For what?"

"I'm having a party this next Saturday. For you and the children."

"That's not necessary."

"Oh but it is. I want to apologize for giving up on being Santa all these years."

"That's okay, Henri. You can't stand out in the cold anymore."

The smell of heated milk drew her back to the kitchen to stir the pan of cocoa.

He coughed again. "Would your Rudolph behave indoors? How about those goats? If I had somebody make a little pen would they be okay? They're all invited to the party, too."

Henri's eyes twinkled exactly like Peter's when he had danced with her in the barn.

"You really do want the kids and animals at your house for a party, don't you?"

"Damn straight."

Then she caught on. Her heart sank a little. "The last hurrah before you sell it?"

His face went flaccid. "Already sold it."

"Who bought it?"

"A corporation."

Any bit of life in her core iced over. The era of the LeBarron's was done. Somehow the mayor had won. And Peter had allowed it to happen.

She had to hand it to Henri LeBarron. He knew how to throw a party. A week later, on a brilliantly sunny day, the first floor of the mansion had been draped with ivy garlands, red bows, and mechanical toys on every shelf. A holiday tree sat in the middle of the entry reception hall under the chandelier. Its branches held what seemed to be hundreds of small, wrapped gifts for all the children, which they were invited to pluck off the tree and open every half hour. Crystal had never seen such excess.

Two high school boys she recognized from the football team had been hired to help with the games. They wore elf costumes. Lisa Dane, Marcus's mother, volunteered to help clean up after the party. Mortified by what her husband had done, Lisa said it was important to make amends and treat Crystal to this party. Crystal hugged her, reassuring her that bygones can be bygones.

Leonard Moline, not any less creepy in an elf costume, hurried in and out with trays of Christmas cookies, lemon bars, peppermint ice cream, and cocoa. For the main meal they had macaroni and cheese with hotdogs, which Crystal suspected nearly killed the snooty Leonard to make.

When Crystal tried to help, Leonard told her sternly she was to enjoy the party. He had strict orders from Henri to make sure she had a comfortable chair in the front hall to watch the goings on. He also brought her a dozen roses in a vase to sit nearby, a cup of sweet tea to drink, and warm slippers, the latter a gift from Henri.

Not used to this treatment, she was starting to get suspicious. Why was Henri treating her like a queen?

Crystal sat back to watch the pony rides inside the house while snow flurries eddied past the windows outside. Leonard followed the pony with a dust pan to catch any of the "road apples", as Henri called them.

In a wheelchair today, Henri rolled next to her. "You're usually the one doing for others. I suppose it's an odd posture for you, sitting still."

"Odd indeed," she said, discovering truth in the old man's words. "I rarely sit down, and even when I do, I have school things to read or work on."

"It's mighty fine to feel out of sorts for once. A little change is good."

"Speaking of which, I swear I heard Leonard talk to you about a Santa costume."

Henri grinned. "Shh. Not so loud. I should be helping Leonard look for that old suit. Not sure where we put it." He began wheeling away.

"Do you want me to help find it? Help you up the stairs?"

"No, no, that won't be necessary." Then Henri flashed her the biggest smile. "I believe I hear the stamp of reindeer feet outside now. Maybe the real Santa's here."

She looked at him. Had he gone daft? But then she heard bells. Lots of them.

Racing to the front door, she flung it open and there on the lawn was Santa Claus in a sleigh with eight reindeer in harnesses.

"Better get your coat, honey," Henri said, "because I think that son of mine means to take you for a ride."

"Peter?" She wriggled into her coat as she shuffled through the deep snow of the front lawn. Her knees quaked at the sight of those eyes hidden under the white costume beard and eyebrows. "What are you doing here?"

"This is the North Pole, isn't it? Where else would you find Santa and his reindeer?"

"Where did you get these reindeer?"

"The mayor found them. I told him we need to spice up the holiday activities around the Square. Where's Rudolph? Bring the poor guy out to join the crew."

Giggling over the surprise of Peter coming back, her body humming with pleasure, she hurried to get Rudolph. He hopped about when he spotted the other reindeer and pawed at the snow after she attached him--her--to the lead position.

Then she smiled at Peter. "You don't know what you're doing with these animals at all, do you?"

"Not one iota. We almost crashed into a bush out by the street. I figure you'll teach me. Did you know these animals can fly at up to fifty miles an hour?"

"Where'd you learn that?"

"From my father. Now get in."

She hurried aboard the small sleigh. Peter kept the reins, insisting he wanted to learn. Fortunately, the caribou were well-trained. They began pulling Peter and Crystal toward the back of the mansion and the moonscape of snow. Crystal's heart thrilled as she looked at Peter under the Santa costume. His dark eyes radiated with reflections of the sunlight on snow. She'd forgotten her mittens, but she didn't even need them, what with the flush of excitement coursing inside her.

The sleigh eased over the drifts. With the deep snow, Rudolph and the other caribou took their time.

"What's really going on?" she asked.

"I had to come back to tell you something I learned from you. And learned from my father about you."

"All the way from eighty-degree Phoenix? A phone call could've done that."

The bells jingled. Santa laughed on the frosty afternoon air. "You don't just care about your kids and the people of Moonstone. You have a deep respect for what goes on here. And when things go wrong, you dig in. You don't leave."

She tried to object but he wouldn't let her. They made a wide circle in the yard. Peter was getting the hang of the reins and signals. Crystal now had a rare view of the magnificent mansion's portico that faced the lake. Its beauty rendered her speechless.

"You expect great things of people," Peter said. "But you need to expect more respect."

Peter made no sense.

"I heard about Randy," he said. "My father couldn't wait to tell me."

"He was just being Randy."

"See? There you go again. Forgiving people so easily. Always the angel, forgiving everybody. You should be mad at that guy. It's why I came back."

"So you could fight him?"

"Because you need somebody watching out for you. And I'm your man."

A thrill zipped up her spine. Did she hear him right? "I thought some corporation bought this place. I thought you weren't coming back."

"A corporation did indeed buy it. One run by me. You have to incorporate if you're going to run a Christmas shop and fine dining establishment out of the North Pole."

"You're turning this into a restaurant? A gift shop?" Her mind swirled as if she were inside a snow globe and somebody had shaken her.

"I can see you don't get it. Hang on."

With that he called to his reindeer and they turned yet again to fly fast over the snow and out onto the frozen lake. When they were maybe a hundred yards away from the mansion, he pulled the reindeer around again and stopped them. They pranced in place, puffing steam.

Crystal had a breathtaking view of the North Pole. From here the tall pine trees framed the estate. A few boulders on the shoreline gave the landscape its unique character. With the sweeping lawn now covered with snow, the house with its green roof and red trim did indeed look like the North Pole to Crystal.

Peter stared at the mansion. "I took a walk out here the night before I left. My father had mentioned that the condos would go in the flower beds my mother used to plant. I realized how much my father loved my mother. She was unhappy in her life, but not about this. I can't blame my father for what happened. He built this for my mother. He loved her that much."

The enormity of that registered with Crystal.

"I figure we could rent out the lawn for parties, though we could serve dinner outside, too. Of course we have to revive my mother's flower beds."

She noticed the "we" in his speech. More of his usual flirtations?

Peter went on. "My father will still live upstairs and oversee everything, though I think I've convinced him he may need to move."

"Why is that? I thought you two were getting along better."

"Oh, we are. Because of you. But he'll have to move because you and I need our privacy."

She swallowed. "You're going through a midlife crisis, aren't you?"

"I just might be. But men of my age usually opt for a shiny red roadster. What do you make of a man who buys a sleigh and reindeer to travel in? Why would he do such a thing?" His eyes deepened, as if they were fashioned from the molten core of the earth. He took off the Santa hat and beard and eyebrows.

Crystal didn't want to bring this up, but she had to help him face the truth. "Peter, have you ever thought that your father was behind everything? That maybe he paid Lowell Dane to steal Rudolph and bring you and me together? Don't you wonder if you've been manipulated? To save this estate? After all, you said it. This is where he loved your mother beyond belief. Henri would do anything to save this place."

"I suspected him of matchmaking myself. And you know what?" Peter took off his mittens, then caressed her face in his warm palms. "I realized, all on my own, that I didn't care. I realized this past week how much I missed dancing with you in your barn. With you, I felt whole again. Actually, I was feeling again, not just operating on autopilot."

With fire leaping through her veins, she still couldn't quite trust the words or the intensity in his eyes. "Why are you really back?"

With a thumb he caressed the corner of her mouth. "My father asked me what got me up every morning. I have big accomplishments but they have never been personal to me. I manage millions of dollars for businesses and other individuals, but, so what? You and my father have the power to change a whole town. My father has the power to put people out of work, or help them find new jobs. And you control Christmas, for cryin' out loud. That's what they'll put in your obituary some day. I push paper, you push hearts. Kids love you."

"Peter--"

He pressed his thumb over her lips, his heat stilling her. "You didn't go to lunch with me that day to negotiate for Rudolph, for example. You went there to be sure Michael was dealing okay with his father's absence. I saw the tears leave your eyes when you watched that little boy on my shoulders forgetting his troubles for a few minutes. After I returned to Phoenix, I didn't have kids wanting me to give them a ride. There was no woman asking me to help her find Rudolph."

"But that's all I am or will be. A woman living in a small town."

"You made me feel worth something for a weekend. Maybe this is a midlife crisis. How else do I explain falling in love over the course of a weekend and because of a kidnapped reindeer?"

Crystal put a hand over her heart to keep it from leaping out of her chest. *Did he just say he loved me? Does he mean it?*

Leaning toward her so that she saw her own reflection in his eyes, Peter whispered, "I knew I loved you the moment you brought over the chocolate pudding cake. I'd be a fool not to ask you to marry me."

If a heart could sprout wings, hers just did. "My toes are wiggling inside my boots."

"A good sign? They're not cold, are they?"

"I'm very, very hot," she said, "for you, and my toes are saying 'yes, I'll marry you'. Peter LeBarron, I love you, too."

And then Santa caressed her in a way that even embarrassed the reindeer, forcing Rudolph to lead them home to the North Pole before the children spotted Santa kissing their teacher.

If you enjoyed this author's book, then please place a review up at the site of purchase, and any social media sites you frequent!

You can find ALL our books on our website at:

http://www.writers-exchange.com

All our romances:

http://www.writers-exchange.com/category/genres/romance/

All Christine's Books:

http://www.writers-exchange.com/christine-desmet/

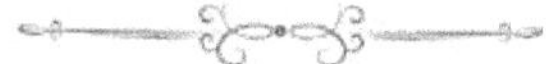

About the Author

Christine DeSmet is an award-winning fiction writer and professional screenwriter. She is the author of the bestselling *Fudge Shop Mystery Series* and the popular novella series called *Mischief in Moonstone.*

She is a Distinguished Faculty Associate in Writing at University of Wisconsin-Madison where she teaches novel writing and screenwriting and directs the annual summer Write-by-the-Lake Writer's Workshop & Retreat. Through her master classes she has seen many of her adult students become published.

She is also a professional writing coach in the UW-Madison Writers' Institute conference's Pathway to Publication program.

Christine is a member of Mystery Writers of America, Sisters in Crime, Wisconsin Writers Association, Wisconsin Screenwriters Association, and other professional associations.

Christine is active on Facebook and you can also find her at http://www.ChristineDeSmet.com

Christine's author page at Writers Exchange E-Publishing is: http://www.writers-exchange.com/christine-desmet/

If you want to read more about books by this author, they are listed on the following pages...

Fudge Shop Mystery Series

Deadly Fudge Divas

A taste of trouble is in the air when a group of well-heeled, fudge-loving women descend on Ava Oosterling's newly acquired and lovingly refurbished bed & breakfast inn for a chocolate lovers' getaway.

When one of the women turns up dead--and Ava's grandfather is a prime suspect--Ava plunges into the thick of a murder case stickier than her candy store's line of Fairy Tale fudge flavors and the chocolate facials the women adore at the local spa.

It's springtime and the start of the tourist season in Fishers' Harbor, Wisconsin. Ava has opened the Blue Heron Inn with the help of handsome construction worker Dillon Rivers. Unfortunately, Dillon's mother--Ava's ex-mother-in-law--is among the secretive divas who become suspects along with Grandpa.

Ava turns for help from her friends but they have troubles, too. One is eager for a wedding proposal to unfold on live television, while another friend is expecting her first baby and asks Ava to assist with the birth.

Everything and everybody Ava loves seems in chaos--her fudge shop, her inn, her family, and her own friendships... Until she uncovers a thirty-year-old secret of the "deadly fudge divas".

Publisher: https://www.writers-exchange.com/deadly-fudge-divas/

Undercover Fudge

Candy shop owner Ava Oosterling has her hands full when her best friend Pauline Mertens takes a summer job as a wedding coordinator--with the nuptials and reception scheduled in mere days in the back yard of Ava's Blue Heron Inn overlooking Lake Michigan's bay.

To help out her best friend, Ava is intent on making the table favors-- edible fudge lighthouses patterned after their county's 11 lighthouses.

Unfortunately, trying to finish the luscious ruby chocolate lighthouses becomes elusive. The sheriff informs Ava that a band of thieves storming the country may have targeted this wedding. And that's because there's proof Pauline's mother is associated with the thieves.

When the sheriff asks Ava to go undercover, she finds herself in an emotional quagmire. Pauline's mother only recently returned to Fishers' Harbor after years of estrangement from her daughter. And, Coletta Mertens now works as the housekeeper at Ava's inn. Has Ava's fudge-and-wine hospitality provided a hideout for a criminal?

Unfortunately, "until death do us part" takes a murderous twist involving Ava's Grandpa Gil, the dog Lucky Harbor, and Ava's own beau.

Publisher: https://www.writers-exchange.com/undercover-fudge/

Holly Jolly Fudge Folly

An early, deep snow has gifted Fishers' Harbor, Wisconsin, with a perfect setting for the holiday celebration. Unfortunately removing snow from Main Street for the parade reveals the dead tax assessor with a knife in him-- containing Grandpa Gil's fingerprints.

It's clearly a setup and one that keeps Ava and Grandpa Gil under the watchful eyes of Sheriff Tollefson. Who wants Grandpa to miss playing Santa Claus in the Christmas parade and why? Who's being naughty instead of nice?

Grandpa doesn't help his case with talk of leaving town for good--words that chill Ava worse than the weather. She can't imagine life without Grandpa's warm hugs and laughter.

When vandals strike the historic shop and someone leaves Ava and fiancé Dillon Rivers for dead in the snow, Ava wonders if she may need the magical help of Santa's elves to solve the holiday folly.

Publisher: https://www.writers-exchange.com/holly-jolly-fudge-folly/

Mischief in Moonstone Series

Nestled against the sparkling shores of Lake Superior, the tiny village of Moonstone is anything but ordinary. Between romantic entanglements, quirky neighbors, and mysteries that seem to pop up with every season, the locals know life here comes with a generous dose of laughter and surprise. From silkie chickens and a giant prehistoric beaver skeleton to kidnapped reindeer and holiday hijinks, mischief is always waiting just around the corner. Fall in love with the humorous, heartwarming adventures of Moonstone--where romance meets mayhem in the most delightful ways.

Novella 1: When Rudolf was Kidnapped

Crystal Hagan's first-graders are in panic mode. Their beloved holiday reindeer, Rudolph, has been stolen from the school's live Christmas display. Without him, the children are convinced Christmas is canceled.

The trail of mischief leads to Peter LeBarron, the wealthy recluse who lives in a mansion locals call the "North Pole." To Crystal's shock, Peter freely admits to taking Rudolph--but he refuses to give him back without some romantic negotiations of his own.

With the holiday countdown ticking, Crystal must juggle her students' worries, a stolen reindeer, and an unexpected suitor who may have just stolen her heart.

Humorous, heartwarming, and filled with small-town Christmas magic, this novella is perfect for fans of cozy romance and holiday cheer.

Publisher: https://www.writers-exchange.com/when-rudolph-was-kidnapped/

Novella 2: Misbehavin' in Moonstone

Kirsten Peplinski has worked hard to open her dream restaurant on the shores of Lake Superior. But when the men of Moonstone start disappearing in the evenings--and her business suffers--she discovers the shocking reason: a touring boat offering topless entertainment just outside town limits.

Determined to put an end to the mischief, Kirsten confronts the boat's infuriatingly handsome owner, Jonathon VanBrocklin. Instead of backing down, Jonathon kidnaps her--claiming undressing and marriage are the only items on his menu.

Caught between outrage and unexpected attraction, Kirsten faces the wildest adventure of her life. Will she escape this reckless scheme, or discover that true love sometimes arrives in the most mischievous packages?

Humorous, romantic, and funny, cheeky, and charming, *Misbehavin' in Moonstone* is a sizzling small-town escape.

Publisher: https://www.writers-exchange.com/misbehavin-in-moonstone/

Novella 3: Mrs. Claus and the Moonstone Murder

New county deputy Lily Schuster is still learning the ropes when trouble strikes in Moonstone, Wisconsin. On her second day, she arrests archaeologist Marcus Linden for trespassing--only to find herself turning to him for help when a pie contest judge ends up murdered.

The suspects? None other than Henri LeBarron, the town's beloved eighty-four-year-old Santa, and his scandalous new companion, the alluring Felicity Starr. Both women are vying to become "Mrs. Claus" for the upcoming winter celebration--and their rivalry has turned deadly.

With August heat bearing down and tempers flaring, Lily must solve the case, keep her wits about her, and decide if Marcus's kisses are worth more than his alibis.

Quirky, romantic, and full of small-town mischief, *Mrs. Claus and the Moonstone Murder* blends mystery with a heart-stealing romance.

Publisher: https://www.writers-exchange.com/mrs-claus-and-the-moonstone-murder/

Novella 4: When the Dead People Brought a Dish-to-Pass

Three days before Halloween, Alyssa Swain finds a dead man in his car. But when she returns with help, the body has vanished.

Things only get stranger when the supposed corpse--scruffy, tall John Christopherson--appears on her doorstep very much alive...or at least claiming to be. John insists she summoned him to help prepare for a Halloween party, and he refuses to leave her house--or her heart.

But midnight on Halloween looms, and Alyssa must find a way to keep John from crossing into the afterlife forever.

Funny, eerie, and tender, When the Dead People Brought a Dish-to-Pass is a paranormal romance that blends small-town charm with Halloween magic.

Publisher: https://www.writers-exchange.com/when-the-dead-people-brought-a-dish-to-pass/

Novella 5: A Moonstone Wedding

Margie Mueller thought wedding jitters were normal--until her fiancé sent her a fertility rug.

She's no spring chicken, and the idea of raising a brood of Farina babies makes her panic. But before she can call the whole thing off, Tony's boisterous family descends on Moonstone with their parties, opinions, and endless interference.

Then a dead man turns up--wrapped in that same fertility rug. Suddenly, Margie's wedding isn't just in danger of collapsing under family chaos--it's at the center of a murder mystery. And Tony may know more than he's admitting.

Funny, quirky, and laced with small-town mischief, A Moonstone Wedding is a romantic novella with a deadly twist.

Novella 6: The Moonstone Fire

John "Bozeman" Hall has seen it all--longhorn cattle, grizzly hunts, even rattlesnake suppers. But nothing prepares him for Moonstone, Wisconsin.

When a suspicious fire destroys the newlyweds Crystal and Peter LeBarron's farm cabin, Bozeman is determined to track down the arsonist. His first suspect? A young homeless mother and her son, squatting in a cave on the property.

But the closer he gets to the truth, the more Bozeman discovers that danger isn't the only spark in town--so is the pull of unexpected love.

The Moonstone Fire delivers a sizzling blend of small-town mystery, heartwarming romance, and the quirky mischief Moonstone is known for.

Publisher: https://www.writers-exchange.com/the-moonstone-fire/

Coming November 2025...

Novella 7: All She Wore Was a Bow

Kincaid Hunter, professional bull rider and decorated veteran, has never been tamed--least of all by the thought of marriage. But when a good friend back home in Wisconsin plans a Christmas wedding, Kincaid can't resist riding in to try and stop him from making what he thinks is a big mistake.

What Kincaid doesn't expect is to be lassoed himself--by a wedding planner dressed as Mrs. Claus, with a sparkle in her eyes and a bow for every occasion.

Soon, the cowboy who vowed he'd never walk down the aisle discovers that love can tie a knot tighter than any rope.

All She Wore Was a Bow is a festive small-town romance full of humor, heart, and holiday magic.

Publisher: https://www.writers-exchange.com/the-moonstone-fire/

Coming Soon:
Novella 8: Pest Control
Novella 9: The Big Love & Murder Shilly-Shally in Moonstone

You can find ALL our books on our website at:

http://www.writers-exchange.com

All our romances:

http://www.writers-exchange.com/category/genres/romance/

All Christine's Books:

http://www.writers-exchange.com/christine-desmet/